## "It appears we've reached an impasse."

Khaled's voice was a low, rich rumble. She remembered that sound: its timbre, its pitch, the perfect English with its precise upper-class diction. What she didn't remember was the curious tingling it sent along her spine. And just whom was he talking to?

She squinted through the gaps in the dressing room doors. Was someone in the lounge beyond the bedroom?

"My car is ready and I need to dress, so either I pretend I don't know you are in there and risk a scene when the door is opened, or you come out now and spare us both the drama."

Lily went hot and cold all at the same time. He knew she was there.

The prince stared at the dressing room, then with an exasperated sigh he strode toward it. The door was flung wide and there he was, staring right at her: taller, broader and so much more *naked* than he'd appeared from behind the safety of the slats.

"Miss Marchant, what a pleasant surprise." His ∙ry tone suggested he felt the exact opposite. "⌐se, do join me."

**Julieanne Howells** loves the romance of a stormy day, which is just as well because she lives in the rainy North East of England. On inclement days, if she's not writing or reading, she has a fondness for cooking. Sometimes her efforts are even edible. She compensates for her lack of domestic skills by being an expert daydreamer, always imagining ways for plucky heroines to upend the worlds of handsome, provoking heroes. For Julieanne, writing for Harlequin is just about the perfect job.

*This is Julieanne Howells's debut book for Harlequin Presents—we hope that you enjoy it!*

# Julieanne Howells

—

## DESERT PRINCE'S DEFIANT BRIDE

**HARLEQUIN**
PRESENTS

ISBN-13: 978-1-335-56937-0

Desert Prince's Defiant Bride

Copyright © 2022 by Julieanne Howells

Recycling programs
for this product may
not exist in your area.

This edition published by arrangement with Harlequin Books S.A.

For questions and comments about the quality of this book, please contact us at CustomerService@Harlequin.com.

Harlequin Enterprises ULC
22 Adelaide St. West, 41st Floor
Toronto, Ontario M5H 4E3, Canada
www.Harlequin.com

Printed in U.S.A.

# DESERT PRINCE'S
# DEFIANT BRIDE

For Paul.

Thank you for the endless encouragement and unfailing belief, for valiantly trying not to glaze over when asked for the hundredth time to reread a scene and, most importantly, for all the years of love and laughter. What more could a girl need in her hero?

# CHAPTER ONE

THE RECEPTION ROOMS of the Surrey mansion were thronged with the great and the good. Not a soul amongst them would have declined the invitation to this charity event. It was worth the cost of the hefty donation alone just to be in the same room as its host: the achingly glamorous Sad Prince.

Officially he was His Royal Highness, Crown Prince Khaled bin Bassam al Azir, but unless addressing him directly, who used his official title? Certainly never the press. They preferred the poignant epithet; it suited him too well.

'Of course it does,' said one of their number, a society columnist holding court amidst a gaggle of guests. 'Can you recall a single image where the Prince is smiling?'

Beside her, the woman's husband shook his head. 'Not a one. Always looks so melancholy, poor devil.'

'Poor? Nabhan may be a desert kingdom, but first there was the oil, and now it's a financial hub. The man's as rich as Croesus. And he's what? Thirty-two? In his prime, with the world at his feet. What's poor about that?'

'I suppose,' her husband said, snagging a glass of champagne from a passing waiter. 'But when does he take time off to enjoy it?'

It was seven years since the King's ill health had forced his retirement from public life. His only son had assumed the workload of prince and monarch, and by all accounts, not stopped working since.

'Things might have been different had the older brother survived that accident, of course,' the husband said mournfully into his glass. 'But who was surprised when it ended badly for him? Always too reckless, that one.'

There were murmurs of agreement from the little group.

*'A horrible business, losing your sibling like that.'*

*'No wonder the Prince looks so tortured.'*

Sensing an unwelcome shift in their attention, the columnist said loudly, 'But have you heard the rumours? Apparently he's about to choose himself a wife.'

There was a collective 'ooh…' and all eyes turned back to her.

'The Palace has denied it, of course, but who believes that? Not when he's been conspicuously single for six months.' She cast a meaningful look around her audience. 'Now there's a man preparing the way for his bride…' Seeing the meat and bones of tomorrow's piece, far more juicy than this dull old charity event, the columnist added, 'And did you notice how he disappeared promptly at eleven? Maybe the girl's actually tucked away here.'

She placed a hand to her bosom and gazed feelingly into the distance.

'We could say we were there the night the Sad Prince proposed to his future princess. Oh, the romance of it.'

'Romance?' her husband scoffed, quite ruining the moment and earning a filthy look from his wife. 'She can forget all that. With that one she'll be lucky to get so much as a smile.'

For the young woman who was indeed hidden away in a private part of the house, the Prince's smile, or lack thereof, was not her most pressing concern. Neither was there any romance in the air.

At that moment, though, the Sad Prince was in his suite and removing his clothes. Far from entertaining some fortunate female he was, in fact, alone.

Lily Marchant knew this for a certainty.

She knew this despite being neither his prospective bride nor his new girlfriend, nor yet being on the guest list for the event still in full swing downstairs. Nor, before this evening, having even set eyes on the man in over a decade.

She knew this because she had a ringside view from her hiding place behind the louvred doors of his dressing room—the only place to suggest itself for concealment at extremely short notice.

The Prince had already slipped off his impeccable dinner jacket. The obligatory bow tie hung loose at the collar of his crisp white shirt. Even now his fingers were going to the buttons, revealing a tantalising glimpse of toned chest.

Lily knew the decent thing would be to look away—the man had no idea he was being observed after all. But this was Prince Khaled al Azir. He of the film-star looks, the heart-stopping sex appeal. And once, before she'd grown up and understood how nonsensical it was, the very epicentre of all her romantic hopes and dreams.

His olive-toned skin and raven-dark hair he'd inherited from his Nabhani-born father. From his English mother came impossibly high cheekbones and deep-set pale grey eyes. The sensuous mouth and the look of cool hauteur were all his own, and he was, quite simply, stunning.

Even with his clothes on.

Lily sneaked closer to the gaps in the doors.

A gold watch fell with a clatter to the bedside table, followed by a pair of cufflinks, their diamond studs glittering in the soft lamplight. Both so casually discarded and probably worth a king's ransom. Certainly more than she or her stepbrother could ever hope to afford.

Lily's mouth tightened as she was reminded of why she was there.

Because of the kind of man the Prince had become.

Ruthless and heartless.

At least enough to abandon his closest friend precisely when he needed his support the most. Meaning Nate had had to turn to her for help.

Lily was still reeling from that morning's phone call.

*'Baby Sis, I'm in trouble and you're the only one I can trust.'*

*Baby Stepsis*, she could have corrected, though it hardly mattered. Nate was all the family she had, or the only one who would acknowledge her, at least.

Her big, handsome stepbrother, whom her friends swooned over. But to her was just Nate, her lifeline, the only person who'd ever tried to put her first.

Whether that had been ditching his own plans to take her shopping for her first grown-up party dress and then being there to collect her after the dance, or rearranging his diary to attend school sports days or prize-givings. The only adult in her life who ever had.

Nate was her hero. She'd help him come what may.

*'Funds have disappeared from the charity account and Khaled thinks I'm responsible,'* he'd told her.

The men had been friends since school. Nate

even worked for him now, as director of the charity benefitting from tonight's event. How could Khaled believe such a thing?

Through the slits in the doors Lily glared at the real villain here. But then off went that snowy white shirt, sliding from a perfectly sculpted back.

The dressing room became rather airless.

She'd seen photographs. Who hadn't? He was one of the most photographed and photogenic men on the planet. She'd even seen him close up before. Twice.

None of that quite prepared a girl for the effect of seeing the man he was now. Though there were traces of the teenage boy she'd once known, this bare-chested Adonis was all power and physical confidence.

As he crossed the room Lily gazed after him— and almost toppled into a row of neatly hung suits. A hanger creaked as it swung on the clothes rail.

The Prince stopped.

Right next to the small table set in the window recess.

Where her stepbrother's laptop now lay.

Where there had been only an *empty* tabletop when she'd entered the suite.

She gnawed on a finger. Why hadn't she brought the wretched thing in here with her?

Frantically she tried to remember Nate's advice should the worst happen.

*'Improvise.'*

*'Improvise how, exactly?'* she'd asked.

*'I don't know... Cry, throw yourself on his mercy, or...'*

She'd waited for something useful.

*'Don't get caught.'*

Don't get caught? When Khaled stood right next to evidence that he had an intruder.

But after trailing a long finger across the computer lid, he turned, disappearing into the bathroom opposite her hideout.

Lily deflated on a long sigh. There was still a chance to get out of this. The Prince was otherwise occupied. From the bathroom came the sound of a shower running.

Nate needed her to get his laptop. He wanted to check for evidence of how the money had been taken. He had his suspicions, he'd said, but he couldn't tell her. Not yet. He didn't think it was safe. Khaled had it with him, and the best chance to retrieve it would be for her to attend the charity event he was hosting.

Penny, Nate's secretary, was on the guest list but had fallen ill. *'You can pretend to be her. If we're lucky no one will check.'*

So Lily had dug out her one good dress, taken the hour-long train journey from London, followed by twenty minutes in a taxi, all the while nervously practising a plausible speech which in the end hadn't even been needed. With the barest of checks, she'd been allowed in.

Accessing the private part of the house had, however, proved to be altogether more difficult.

After mingling on the ground floor she'd sidled towards the main staircase. Only to be halted by a besuited, polite, but totally intimidating guard.

She'd needed a plan B.

A line of French windows had been thrown wide, allowing cooler air to flow in and overheated partygoers to stroll out. Lily had joined them on the terrace where, by luck, she'd found an alternative route to the first floor.

It had been tricky, but she'd actually made it into the Prince's private quarters, and there had sat Nate's laptop, in broad view on the desk.

She'd moved it to the table by the window and, because she'd lost the folding tote she'd brought for the job, had been searching for something to carry it in when she'd heard voices along the corridor.

There'd barely been time to race to the dressing room and close the door behind her before the Prince had walked into his suite.

Now here she was, surrounded by rows of expensive tailoring that had a delicious scent of citrus and spice, wondering how to get out unnoticed.

She almost leapt from her skin at the trilling of the bedside phone.

Khaled reappeared, a towel slung low around his hips. He took the call, looking directly at her hideaway as he spoke. Lily lurched back. Her elbow collided with a row of shoes, catapulting two into the air. She caught them just before they slammed into the door and puffed out her cheeks in silent relief.

Khaled replaced the receiver.

'It appears we've reached an impasse.'

His voice was a low, rich rumble. She remembered that sound: its timbre, its pitch, the perfect English with its precise, upper-class diction. What she didn't remember was the curious tingling it sent along her spine.

And just who was he talking to?

She squinted through the gaps in the doors. Was someone in the lounge beyond the bedroom?

'My car is ready and I need to dress. So either I pretend I don't know you're in there, and risk a scene when the door is opened, or you come out now and spare us both the drama.'

Lily went hot and cold all at the same time.

He knew she was there.

The Prince stared at the dressing room, then with an exasperated sigh strode towards it. The door was flung wide and there he was, staring right at her: taller, broader, and so much more *naked* than he'd appeared from behind the safety of the slats.

'Miss Marchant, what a pleasant surprise.' His icy tone suggested he felt the exact opposite. 'Please, do join me.'

He made no attempt to move aside, so her nose almost brushed his bare chest as she slid from the shadows and into his bedroom.

Blinking in the brighter light, she raised her eyes to the Sad Prince—to six foot three of powerfully built, barely dressed, angry adult male looming over her. He wasn't looking particularly sad right now.

If ever improvisation skills were needed...

'Hello, Khaled,' she said jauntily. 'We must stop meeting like this.'

His brow knotted. 'I don't see any similarity. As I recall, last time it was your cloakroom you were hiding in, and I definitely had not broken into your rooms.'

He reached for the shoes she still clutched.

'I also didn't steal anything from you. What are these for?' He held them aloft before tossing them onto the bed. 'A souvenir of your visit?'

'I'm really sorry, I know I shouldn't be in here, but I got lost trying to find the...the ladies' room.'

One ebony brow lifted, but that beautiful face didn't soften for a moment.

'I genuinely came in here by mistake, and then when I heard you outside I'm afraid I panicked and hid.'

'Indeed?' His fierce gaze didn't waver. 'You were lost and yet you didn't think to ask any of the guards stationed along the corridor for directions?'

'Guards?' Lily swallowed, and shot a glance to the suite doors, imagining the fearsome figure from earlier waiting beyond them.

'Yes, several. Stationed between here and the reception rooms.'

He was still disconcertingly close. Lily watched, fascinated, as a droplet of moisture dripped from his hair to trail in a sinuous pattern down that muscled torso.

She dragged her gaze away. 'If I'd seen them I would certainly have known not to come in here.'

'And had they seen you they would have prevented you from doing so, I assure you.'

'But I saw no one. Perhaps they had slipped away to…to powder their noses, or something?'

The look he bestowed on her was one of pure disdain. 'They're all ex-special forces. I doubt they've powdered a damn thing in their lives.'

Lily could believe it, but thought it wise not to comment.

Arctic grey eyes bored into her. 'So you entered these rooms in error. But please, enlighten me, why were you in my house in the first place?'

He was looming again; her five-four frame was no match for his soaring height.

'For the charity event, of course.' She injected a little disdain of her own into her voice. 'Why else would I be here?'

He folded his arms across that broad chest. He

must work out a lot. Muscles like that were no simple gift of nature.

'You weren't on the guest list and it was invitation-only,' he said.

Ah, this she was prepared for. 'A friend was due to attend, but she's ill. She gave me her ticket. She knew I'd want to come.'

'I see. You have an interest in the cause?'

'Of course,' she lied. Well, she might have if she'd bothered to find out what it was. 'It's such a worthy cause and it's long been close to my heart.'

'The endangered flora and fauna of the Nabhani marshlands?' He looked disbelieving. 'And how long have you supported the charity?'

'Oh, you know,' she said, waving a hand through the air, 'absolutely ages.'

'Miss Marchant, the charity was officially launched this evening.'

She opened her mouth to answer, but nothing sensible came to mind. Except to curse, despite their perilous state, all the beasts and flowers of the marshes of Nabhan. Wasn't it a desert country? How could it have marshland?

'I must have confused it with another charity.'

'Evidently.'

Her weak smile garnered no response. Evidently it was time she got out of there.

'Well, it's been lovely catching up, but I really ought to be going.'

Strong fingers closed about her bare arm. 'I think not.'

The impact of that skin-on-skin contact arrived at her legs just as she required them to move. She was being marched to the lounge area of the suite.

On another occasion she might have admired the tasteful decor, the watered silk wall coverings, the richly hued rugs underfoot, but right now all she could digest was the shocking heat of that touch and the debilitating effect it was having on her ability to walk.

'Sit,' he said, pushing her onto a sofa.

Hardly necessary. Her knees buckled of their own accord.

Khaled snatched up the remote control for a TV standing in the corner of the room. He scrolled through channels until images from a security camera appeared on the screen. The footage showed the exterior of the house, the balcony outside this bedroom, the ivy-clad wall below.

He perched on the desk. Lily tried not to stare at the extra inches of muscular thigh revealed as the towel rode higher.

'So, let's clarify. You claim you are here as a long-time supporter of a charity which was only launched this evening. I find you lurking in my private rooms—which, you maintain, you entered by accident.'

Above the fireplace hung an eighteenth-century hunting canvas. Riders, horses, and a pack of bay-ing hounds streamed across the foreground, whilst in the distance a fox ran for its life.

Empathising with that harried speck of orange, Lily said, 'Yes, of course. I've already explained. I was lost.'

His mouth tightened at her response.

'Then kindly explain this.' He punched a button on the remote.

On screen, the figure of a woman appeared, creeping along the base of the wall. She peered up at the balcony whilst she slipped off her sandals and snagged their straps between her teeth. A clutch bag was tucked down the front of her dress and then—Lily squirmed at this—she hitched up her hem and tucked it up into the legs of her knickers. The woman grasped the ivy and began to climb.

Khaled snorted in disapproval and Lily looked away. She knew what came next.

Halfway up, the climber lost her footing, and as she swung about, fighting to regain her grip, the shoes slipped from her teeth to fall into the rose bed below.

Lily curled her bare toes out of view.

Eventually the woman reached the balcony, heaving herself over, only to scrabble for the bag as it tumbled from her cleavage, joining the missing shoes. Worst of all, the hem of the dress had worked loose, got caught on the railing and hitched higher, revealing, in mortifying detail, an expanse of lace-clad bottom.

Lily slid her fingers across the tell-tale tear in the hem of her dress. She could do nothing about the burning heat of her face.

'She's very enterprising,' she said. 'Is she a groupie or something?'

Khaled stared at her. 'You're actually going to pretend that isn't you?'

She doubted crying or throwing herself on this man's mercy would help. All she had left was bluff.

'You think I could make a climb like——?'

'Enough!'

She jumped as the remote clattered onto the desk. 'I've given you the chance to be honest with me, but it seems you're determined to continue with this nonsense. I don't have time for it. So here are your options. One, we call the police and allow them to get the bottom of this.'

Lily swallowed. 'And option two?'

'We take the more civilised route. I have business in the capital. You agree to come with me. Take some time to consider your position. Then, if you're wise, you'll answer my questions about your stepbrother.'

Right now, anything was better than being arrested.

'I've missed the last train back, so a lift home would be good,' she said. 'I'll go for the second option—though what more we have to discuss I can't imagine.'

An odd, almost triumphant expression crossed his face. 'Finally you show some sense.'

He called out to whoever was waiting on the landing beyond his suite.

A man entered. His black suit was finely tailored, but his solid frame and watchful eyes belonged to a much tougher existence. He was reassuring, or formidable, depending on how you looked at it—and a familiar face Lily realised.

'Hello, Rais,' she said to Khaled's personal bodyguard. The same man who had protected the teenage Prince all those years ago.

He dipped his head in greeting.

'Miss Marchant is coming with us,' Khaled said. 'Take her to the car. I'll be there in five minutes.'

If Rais was surprised by that announcement he didn't show it. He simply waited for Lily to get to her feet and politely stood aside to allow her to walk out of the suite.

At a private side entrance a car waited, its rear door held open by the guard she'd encountered earlier. The heavy thud as it closed, trapping her inside, felt so ominous it took her three fumbling attempts to fasten her seat belt.

Minutes later Khaled joined her. Now in a grey suit and blue shirt, he looked composed and ridiculously handsome, and in with him had come that scent of citrus and spice.

As it swirled around her an odd excitement fluttered low in her belly. She edged closer to the door, to ease that unsettling sensation and to put more space between her and the figure beside her. She'd thought the car impressively large, but now Khaled had climbed in it seemed filled with him.

As they pulled away she cast him a sidelong glance. He was checking messages on his phone. In the darkness its glow cast eerie shadows across those impossible cheekbones. Lily knew it was a trick of the light, but where before he'd appeared stern, now he had that infamous air of melancholy about him.

Maybe there was still a chance to reason with him.

'Perhaps we could come to a compromise?' she said.

No response.

'I admit hiding in your rooms doesn't look good. I'm actually quite embarrassed about it.'

A thumb scrolled upwards, scanning new messages.

'If I can go home tonight, I promise I'll meet you wherever you want in London tomorrow.'

Now he looked up. 'London?'

'You said you have business in the capital,' she said haltingly. Something in his expression had set alarm bells ringing.

'I have. But I meant the capital of my country.'

'Your country?' It was barely a whisper.

'After the stunt you pulled, did you think I'd simply let you go? Whilst your faithless step-brother remains at large? No, if he wants to gain your freedom he'll give himself up. Until he does, I'm keeping you close. And as I'm going home you, Miss Marchant, are coming with me. To Nabhan.'

# CHAPTER TWO

IF A MAN could be made to combust from a mere look then Lily Marchant was doing her damnedest to send him up in flames. From her seat on the opposite side of the cabin, as far from him as it was possible to get on a Gulfstream V, she glowered at him.

The mood he was in, Khaled could have glared right back. They'd almost missed their flight slot because of her nonsense back at the house. She'd had every opportunity to confess, and yet insisted on dragging out that ridiculous charade.

A lost bona fide guest? Did she imagine he was a complete idiot? Perhaps she did—her duplicitous stepbrother apparently had.

Khaled's rage welled up at the reminder of Nate Marchant's duplicity. His closest friend, whom he'd elevated to director of his new charity because of his ability to schmooze millions from the wealthy. He'd never imagined the man would help himself to those millions.

The excuses he'd had to make tonight to cover for his absence…

But beneath the rage lay true hurt: the cold shock of betrayal by a friend who'd become like a brother to him.

A flutter of movement drew his attention back

across the aisle. They'd hit air turbulence and Lily fingers had convulsed around the armrest. Had she'd never flown before?

'This is perfectly normal,' he said kindly. 'We're quite safe.'

His reward was another fulminating glare.

Perhaps she was still smarting from the way she'd been manhandled aboard. Well, he'd make no apology for that. There'd been mere yards between the car and the jet, and still she'd managed to make a fuss. Yelping as a piece of grit dug into the soles of her bare feet, hopping about, making a show of trying to brush it away.

She'd demanded her shoes but, feeling vengeful, he'd ordered that they be disposed of, and he'd told her so, adding that they'd still be on her feet if she hadn't been intent on breaking and entering. When she'd sent him an evil look, as if he was the villain here, the last of his patience had evaporated and he'd hitched her beneath his arm like a piece of baggage and toted her the final few paces to the plane.

He'd have happily hauled her on board like that, too, even with the risk of paparazzi camped out nearby, but the steps had been too narrow. So he'd shifted his grip, swept his arms about her torso and pulled her back against his chest, her naked toes dangling.

As he'd carried her into the cabin she'd felt so slight, her curves more girl than woman. Except where the weight of her breasts had pressed against his arm.

Khaled tugged at his sleeve, still feeling that sweet, warm pressure. Irritated for allowing it even to register.

Frowning, he looked up, and their eyes clashed again. This time, before she turned away, he caught a flash of fear in her expression.

He felt a prickle of guilt. Why? He wasn't to blame for her predicament. Had she not broken into his rooms she'd be safely at home right now.

He massaged the bridge of his nose, eyeing the papers before him—documents he wanted to get through before they landed. At this point on a flight he'd normally be engrossed in work, but tonight his powers of concentration had deserted him—or, more accurately, been hijacked by the young woman sulking in her seat.

'Can I get you anything, sir?'

Stella, the flight attendant, stood beside him. A great favourite of his family, she'd served them since Khaled had been a boy.

She'd presumed on that level of familiarity tonight, admonishing him as he'd set Lily back on her feet inside the jet. To his annoyance, he'd actually blushed.

And now his appetite appeared to have gone the same way as his concentration. 'Nothing, thank you.'

'Then I'll attend to Miss Marchant. She's seems a little…discomforted.'

He watched Stella approach Lily, wishing it had been one of the other stewards on duty tonight. They'd never dare show any reaction to him bringing a woman on board.

But the problem wasn't really that Lily was female. Girlfriends had often joined him on flights. The difference was that they never travelled with him to Nabhan. Other destinations, yes. Wherever his duties took him. Just never to his home. He knew if they did it would be assumed he had serious intentions about the woman.

Always he was careful to keep such speculation to a minimum. Much good it did him. The media seized upon any titbit, real or otherwise, about the Sad Prince.

That blasted moniker—how he despised it, and the endless attention that went with it. Anyway, damn it all, he did smile sometimes. His mother even had a photo to prove it.

But right now he'd never felt less like smiling.

Speculation was rife that he was about to announce his engagement and press attention had intensified—which, in turn, increased the risk of the charity theft becoming public.

How his enemies would love that.

There'd be questions again about his decisions, his choice of friends, whispers about nepotism and corruption. And the loudest dissenter of all, disguised beneath the pretence of loyalty and concern for the country, would be George Hyde-Wallace—his mother's seventy-four-year-old cousin, and Leader of the Council of Families. The Englishman who, in his thirties, had quit British Special Forces to take a post in Nabhan as bodyguard to the young King Bassam, and years later introduced his widowed employer to his beautiful cousin, gaining him the King's grateful patronage.

Intelligent, ambitious, with a genius for politics and a passion for all things Nabhani, he'd risen to a position of great influence in the country. He'd married into one of its senior families, and eventually become the only European ever to serve on the Council.

Hyde-Wallace had been elected leader by the other families a month after the King's first heart attack.

He'd been a thorn in Khaled's side ever since.

Having become related to the crown by marriage, he'd thought to control his young cousin. When he'd found that wouldn't be the case, he'd tried undermining him instead. Speaking against the Prince's reforms. Claiming they would destroy traditional Nabhani values.

But Hyde-Wallace didn't really care about tradition; he cared about power. Khaled's move towards greater democracy would strip that from him.

Many Nabhani people had made donations to

the new charity, but the most substantial had come from Hyde-Wallace. If the theft were discovered he'd be sure to make capital out of it.

And all this when the six-month-long secret negotiations for his marriage were nearing conclusion.

The irony was that the match had been suggested by George. And, much as it irked Khaled to admit it, it was a sound proposition. The daughter of the King of Qaydar had been raised to the royal life, and would be equipped to deal with its demands. More importantly, with her would come much-needed access to water for the remote western reaches of Nabhan, with an agreement to build a new dam in the mountains straddling their shared border.

But the talks had been difficult. Stalled again and again by the King of Qaydar demanding a curb on the Prince's reforming policies. Khaled had quickly recognised that Hyde-Wallace had brokered the alliance to yoke his cousin to a conservative, backward-looking father-in-law.

Once the engagement was announced, no doubt the union would be spun into some great love affair.

*As if.* He would have no truck with sentiment.

While there was deliberately no one at present, Khaled had of course taken lovers. But those relationships had only ever been about mutual companionship and the sating of physical needs. Not long term and never sentimental. Messy, tangled emotions got in the way of the day job, and he wouldn't allow that. Because nothing was more important to him than duty.

How else was he to make amends for the loss of his brother?

Khaled picked up his papers, remembering previous occupants of the seat opposite him. How at this point in a flight they'd be sitting demurely, most likely working. Not disturbing his concentration. And certainly not flouncing away, as soon as the pilot had announced it was safe to do so, to sit as far from him as possible.

His eyes lifted again in Lily's direction, this time to see her chatting with Stella.

From beneath his lashes, Khaled studied her.

She wore a dress of dark green. A lucky choice. It disguised the grubby stains she'd acquired scrambling up the ivy outside his rooms. Yet the shade also complemented her ivory skin and set off the rich auburn tones of her upswept hair.

Khaled snorted. Unkempt, more like. The style was in disarray, and if more evidence of her misspent evening were needed, one cheek sported smudges of dirt.

Now Lily was flicking through a magazine and getting comfortable, lifting her legs to tuck her bare feet beneath her. There was a flash of grimy soles.

And with that simple image Khaled was assaulted with a rush of memories. Memories of a long-ago summer and a skinny girl, all red hair and freckles. Her feet black as a street urchin's as she clambered up trees or ran laughing through the gardens of her stepfather's estate. A girl with scraped knees, dirt on her face, and always grass stains on her clothes.

How long was it since he'd thought of her and how, for two weeks that summer, she'd brought him a measure of peace when he'd thought he'd never know peace again?

The summer they'd lost Faisal.

His bright, brilliant brother.

His reckless brother, they'd said.

Oh, if they but knew...

He closed his eyes and endured the familiar wave of guilt and loss. It never lessened, and why should it. After what he'd done.

He'd been sixteen. Lily seven.

And now...?

He did the maths.

Twenty-three.

Sixteen years older and little had changed. Still climbing, still barefoot, and still with scraped knees.

Khaled looked closer. A gash to her shin that he hadn't noticed before was oozing blood.

He called Stella over, issued instructions, and then, abandoning his work, crossed the cabin to slide into the space opposite Lily.

Her mouth twisted. 'If I'd wanted to talk to you I'd have stayed in my original seat.'

Her expression softened as Stella appeared at his shoulder, presenting him with a towel and placing a bowl of water and first aid provisions on the shelf beside them.

'Your shin is bleeding,' he explained, laying the towel over his lap and tipping disinfectant into the water. 'There's dirt in the wound, too. It'll get infected if we don't attend to it.'

He started rolling back his shirtsleeves.

'I don't need you to do it,' she said crossly. 'I can look after myself.'

She soaked the sponge Stella had left and bent forward to dab at the torn skin.

In that position, in that dress, it was hard for him to ignore the creamy swell of her breasts. He shouldn't be looking. He should be focusing on Lily the burglar, not Lily the woman. Better yet, he should imagine she was still that skinny schoolgirl he'd once known.

But she was not.

When she'd emerged from his dressing room he'd been surprised by the surge of heat as her big hazel eyes had lifted to his. He'd told himself it was the normal reaction of any red-blooded male finding an attractive young woman in his bedroom. He wasn't concerned. It meant nothing.

Except her floral perfume teased him. It had

clung to his clothes after he'd carried her on board and now it invaded his senses again.

She rose to soak the sponge in fresh water. Her teeth worried at her bottom lip as she worked. Her full, sensuous lip of dusky pink...

Khaled cleared his throat. 'You're lucky that you only have a cut or two. You could have been badly injured on that damn fool climb,' he said.

She shrugged. 'It's just a few scratches. Anyway, Nate needed my help,' she answered, not looking at him.

She bent forward again. This time he sent his gaze to the safety of the carpet.

'What exactly has your stepbrother told you? And don't even think of lying. My patience is wearing thin.'

She looked up at him. 'That there's money missing from the charity fund and you believe Nate is responsible—which is crazy. You know him. He doesn't care about money.'

'That's because he's never been without it before. He lost everything when his father's fortunes collapsed. There was nothing left for either of you, I understand?'

'I don't see what it's got to do with you, but, no, there was nothing. Even the house is to be sold. I moved out two days ago.'

Moved out? Did she have somewhere to go?

There was an unpleasant tightening in his chest. *Get a grip*, he thought, and responded sharply. 'It has everything to do with me if it becomes a motive for theft.'

'However bad it got, Nate would never steal.'

'There is compelling evidence that suggests otherwise.'

She shuffled forward to perch on the edge of her seat, checking for remaining scratches. Helplessly, Khaled's gaze travelled the length of her body from pale shoulder to slender ankle.

*Hell.*

'Have you considered that someone is trying to frame him? Or that actually it's you they're trying to hurt?'

He gave a wry, mirthless laugh. 'Lily, I'm a political leader introducing reform in a region that clings to its traditions. I have numerous enemies. That's why I'm careful to protect myself, and my interests, and why it's almost impossible that anyone other than Nate has the money.'

'*Almost* impossible, but not completely? Then I know Nate is innocent.'

'The transfer originated in his office.'

'Maybe his secretary did it.'

'Penny? Her alibi is solid. Plus, she's worked for the family for years. Even for my mother's cousin for a while. She's beyond reproach.'

Lily shifted again, this time checking the inside of her calf.

He gritted his teeth. He was *not*, he reminded

himself, attracted to short, troublesome redheads, and he'd prove it.

He snatched the sponge from her hand. 'You're not being thorough enough. I'll do it.'

As his fingers touched the soft skin at the back of her knee a shot of pure energy raced straight to his groin. He masked his reaction by carefully checking each scrape for dirt and then reaching for tape and bandages. She'd gone very still, and when she spoke her voice was less certain than it had been.

'Then there is…is some other explanation. Are you even looking for anyone else?'

He gently pressed a lint pad against her skin and secured the edge with tape.

'Not yet. There would be no point.'

'Then you're letting the real culprit get away. You're a fool.'

He stuck on the last pieces of tape and lifted his fingers from her skin, disregarding how he instantly missed its warmth, concentrating instead on her impertinence.

'Says the woman who believed she could gatecrash a private party and not be discovered from the start?'

She watched him, a faint line creasing her brow. He saw the exact moment the penny dropped.

'You knew I was in your dressing room. Even before the phone call.'

'Did you imagine it would be that easy to enter

my home? That a prince of Nabhan would be so little protected? Besides, you made so much noise the entire household would have known you were there.'

He didn't mention that her scent had lingered, too. That he'd picked up on the unfamiliar fragrance the moment he'd entered his suite. She made a hopeless burglar.

She ignored his last remark, clearly caught up in another idea altogether. 'You knew I was there and yet you…you…' She flushed—presumably at the memory of him undressing. She even had the audacity to sound indignant.

'You break into a man's private rooms and expect the social niceties to be observed? I'm on a strict schedule. I had to be ready to leave. I imagined that for decency's sake you would reveal yourself before, shall we say, I did.'

The fabric of her dress suddenly held deep fascination for her, and she plucked at the hem. 'Why did you allow me to break in?'

'I wanted to know what you were searching for.' He invested his voice with the full force of royal authority. 'And now would be a good time to tell me.'

She remained stubbornly silent.

'I know you were there for the laptop.'

She stared at him.

'Lily, you'd moved it to the table by the window. We have the folded bag you brought with you to carry it away in. Who brings a shopping bag to a party? We presume your stepbrother sent you to access something on the hard drive. What was it?'

Her chin came up.

'If Nate had wanted you to know that, he would have told you himself. Obviously he doesn't trust you, and neither do I.'

She was going to defy him? Again?

He was hit with several emotions at once: incredulity, anger, and a sudden, irrational urge to reach over and stop her impertinent little mouth with his own.

It was not good that she'd wound him up to that extent. Time to wrestle back control—in particular of his wayward hormones.

'In that case I think you should prepare yourself for a long stay in Nabhan.'

'How lovely,' she mocked. 'It's ages since I've had a holiday.'

'It won't, I assure you, be any kind of a holiday. That would suggest the freedom to come and go as you please. Which will not be permitted.'

'Why not just throw me in prison and have done with it?'

'Don't tempt me,' he muttered.

Then he took a breath. This was achieving nothing. He forced himself to calm down.

'Before we arrive in Nabhan I think we should set a few ground rules,' he said, as pleasantly as he could.

Lily eyed him suspiciously.

'Under the circumstances, it's hardly appropriate that you should meet any members of my family. So I've—'

'Might they be tainted by my criminal presence?'

Damn it—now she was interrupting him. 'Whilst you have a point,' he snapped back, 'you know that's not what I meant. This is not a social visit. I thought perhaps, both for your sake and Nate's, you would appreciate as much discretion as possible.'

She opened her mouth to reply, but then closed it again, perhaps recognising the sense in keeping this whole sorry affair quiet.

'I've arranged for you to stay in an apartment in Nabhan city. It's on the waterfront and has its own staff. You'll be quite comfortable.'

'You could have shown this level of concern before you dragged me halfway round the world,' she said.

'And you should remember your trip would have been unnecessary had you stayed away from my home or if you'd told me where Nate is. You'll be free to go as soon as you tell me what I want to know or he comes forward.'

'So I'm being kidnapped? Surely even a prince can't just take a woman against her will.'

His temper flared again.

'*Habiba*, trust me—if I were to "take" you, not

only would you be willing, but you'd be begging me for more.'

Her jaw fell open. As well it might. What had possessed him to say something so outrageously inappropriate? He needed to end this conversation.

He stood abruptly, rolling down his shirtsleeves.

As if that was going to dignify his last remark.

'It's late and we still have several hours before we land. I have work to complete,' he said, staring down his nose at her, trying to regain some authority before he went back to his seat. 'I suggest you try and get some rest.'

And before she could throw another impertinence at him he turned away.

# CHAPTER THREE

THE LIGHTS WERE DIMMED. Rais and his team dozed at the rear of the plane. This was the smallest of the royal jets, with no bedroom. Khaled never needed one. He mostly worked during a flight. But in the last ten minutes he'd read the same page a dozen times. Nothing had sunk in. His gaze kept travelling back to where Lily was stretched out on her seat.

Miraculously, she'd done as she was told.

Stella had reclined the seat and converted it into a bed. Now his additional passenger was curled beneath a cashmere blanket, asleep. Her head rested on a plump pillow, but the throw had slipped from her shoulders.

Khaled went to her. He gently tucked the blanket back in place. She murmured and snuggled further beneath its warmth.

He was filled again with the strangest emotions. An odd mix of anger and protectiveness—and something else he felt it wise to ignore.

There were purple shadows beneath her eyes. How many late nights had she endured recently?

Before his death last month, she'd acted as housekeeper to her stepfather. They hadn't been close. Edward Marchant had viewed the young

Lily as an encumbrance, and the older version as cheap labour.

Had she known the extent of his financial difficulties? Had it been a surprise when, essentially, she'd lost her job and home in one day?

In the decade since they'd last met, how had she fared? Because her stepbrother was a close friend of the royal family, Khaled's people would have performed regular background checks on her as a matter of course, but nothing had ever been brought to his notice.

Long dark lashes swept low over pale cheekbones where those smudges of dirt still sat. Her ruined hairstyle even sported a withered ivy leaf. Khaled moved to pluck it clear and found his fingers tangled in silky tresses. They lingered, gently twining one loose curl.

Lily Marchant...

In all kinds of trouble, not really of her own making.

What was it her stepbrother needed so badly that he was prepared to expose her to danger?

There was a sound from the galley. Stella was watching him.

He straightened, felt his cheeks heat. 'Please find Miss Marchant another blanket. It's cool in here,' he ordered, retreating to the safer territory of his own seat.

He snatched up his discarded work, determined to finally make headway.

His efforts were fruitless. Lily held all his attention.

She was in her twenties now, but beneath all her bravado there were traces of that lonely little girl with the heartbreaking air of vulnerability he remembered from that winter…the second and only other time they'd met.

She'd been thirteen—one year younger than his sisters were now and far too young to lose her mother.

Once a feted actress, Niamh had been thirty-three when she'd succumbed to her alcohol addiction. The more romantic version was that it had been the weariness of a broken heart that simply wouldn't heal. Lily's father—dead over a decade by then—had, they said, been mourned to distraction by his beautiful widow.

Lord Rupert Hastings had been a world class eventer, but when a terrible fall had left his spine fused with pins and metal plates he'd been told to retire, or risk death. He'd ignored all pleas to quit, even those of his wife, who had begged him on behalf of their young daughter.

The inevitable had happened.

Niamh's second marriage, so soon after the accident that had ended her first, had been a disaster.

Widower Edward Marchant, who'd inherited his wealth from Nate's mother, had thought he'd married the perfect trophy wife. A famous actress with the added cachet of a connection to a titled family. Once he'd discovered she'd been disowned by her former in-laws and was little more than a heartbroken creature, he'd neglected her, leaving her to seek solace, then oblivion, in a vodka bottle.

When Niamh had died so suddenly Nate, abroad and unable to get home in time, had begged Khaled to go to Lily on his behalf.

'You know she and my father aren't close, and she still talks about you all the time. You're in England at the moment. Be her big brother for a few hours?'

Khaled had remembered the little girl with the kind heart and sunny smile. In all conscience he'd known he couldn't leave her alone on such a day.

His people had worked miracles, carving a few hours from his packed schedule, but even they hadn't conjured up enough time for him to attend the funeral itself. For which, to his lasting shame, he'd been grateful.

It would have been too vivid a reminder of a similar day, six years previously.

The day they'd buried Faisal…

In the cabin, Lily stirred in her sleep. The dim light caught in her hair, a wave of red-gold against the white of the pillow.

His work forgotten, Khaled recalled the girl he'd found that day in her stepfather's house. Alone. Ignored by everyone at the wake. Hiding in a cloakroom, her face buried in the line of coats.

She'd jerked upright when the door had opened.

Someone had tried to smarten her up in a neat black coat, and to tame that riot of auburn hair by squashing a black beret firmly on her head. It had only made her look paler. More out of place. More lost.

His heart had gone out to her.

She'd blinked at him in confusion, then flung herself at his chest, sobbing as if her heart were breaking. He'd pulled her close, wrapping his arms around her, murmuring soft words in Arabic—words she wouldn't understand, and yet they'd seemed to soothe her as the racking sobs had subsided.

Later, they'd sat together in her mother's neglected rose garden and he'd asked her where she'd go now.

She'd looked up at him, puzzled. 'I'll stay here, of course.'

Her stepfather had become her legal guardian. Her mother had even changed Lily's surname when she'd married him. If Edward Marchant had been hoping her father's aristocratic family would claim her he was to be disappointed.

They'd cut all ties when their younger son Rupert had, in their opinion, married beneath him. They were an ancient family, and proud—too proud to accept a mere actress as their daughter-in-law, however celebrated. And at their head was the most intransigent of them all, the Duke, who had steadfastly refused to recognise his own grandchild.

'The only one who's ever pleased to see me is Nate,' she'd told him. 'He's my family now.'

'But who will look after you?' he'd asked. 'Nate's hardly ever home.'

'I'll look after myself. Like I've always done,' she'd said, adding hurriedly, when she saw his shocked expression, 'And there's Mrs Stone.'

He'd remembered the housekeeper from his last visit. Sour-faced and ill-tempered. Hardly the embodiment of maternal tenderness.

'I'll have clean clothes. I'll be fed. She'll get me to school on time.'

There'd been a dismissive shrug, as if to say that was enough.

Enough? For a parentless child?

It had been a dire prospect, and when he'd left that day he'd wanted to scoop her up and take her with him.

'I can't arrive at the airport looking like this.'

The voice of the adult Lily cut through Khaled's reverie. She stood barefoot in the aisle, fiddling with the torn hem of her dress. Outside the sky was bright with sunshine. They were less than half an hour from landing.

'I look like I've been partying all night.'

The tender feelings evaporated. The girl might have evoked his compassion. Not the woman.

They'd been forced together because of her attempted burglary. But she had a point. He wanted a low-key arrival.

A white dress shirt was retrieved from his luggage, and Stella leant her a pair of leather sandals.

The shirt swamped her. It fell almost to her knees and her hands were lost in the sleeves. But once she'd rolled them back, and knotted the shirt-tails at her waist, she looked more presentable. She'd tidied her hair, removed the dirt from her cheeks. It would do.

Besides, they'd disembark far from the public terminals of the airport, and his team would spirit her away to the anonymous apartment. Few people would see her. Fewer still would know that she was here as his 'guest'. Essentially as a hostage to her stepbrother's betrayal.

For now, Nate's stepsister sat quietly in her seat, looking anywhere but at him.

*Good.*

Judging by his inconvenient reaction to her over the last few hours, it would be wise to put some distance between them. He'd be free of her company in about thirty minutes, and while he waited for Nate to be caught, and the money returned, there would be no need for further contact between them. This disturbing episode could be forgotten.

He relaxed, picked up the report he'd been trying to read throughout the flight, and was finally rewarded by the return of his errant concentration.

In front of the airport's private terminal a dozen men in sharp grey suits and mirrored sunglasses stood in strict formation around a motorcade of five cars. At its centre were two shiny black limousines with darkened windows. Their royal pennants fluttered in the breeze.

Khaled swore.

*Not* the anonymous four-by-fours he'd ordered.

'A change of plan, Miss Marchant.'

'Oh? I hope it's inconvenient for you,' she said tartly, from the other side of the plane.

'I'm afraid it will be inconvenient for us both,' he said, as he watched a woman step from one of the cars.

He knew in that instant that his plan to discreetly install Lily in the waterfront apartment was foiled. For out there waited the one person who would always happily interfere in his life—without doubt precisely why she was here now. Though why had she chosen to meet what was supposed to be a routine arrival?

Stella bustled past, gathering blankets and pillows to stow away. She saw his suspicious look. Blinked at him. This time it was she who blushed as she disappeared to the rear of the plane.

Of course. The family favourite had called ahead.

For the first time ever he'd brought a woman with him to Nabhan, and the figure out there, with her romantic notions, would be gleefully jumping to all the wrong conclusions.

He looked to the heavens. Was he to be beset with meddlesome females?

Lily dropped into the seat opposite his. She peered at the scene on the Tarmac for a moment. Looked more closely. Then blenched.

'Is that who I think it is?'

'Yes.' He sighed, getting to his feet. 'Unfortunately it's exactly who you think it is.'

He smoothed his shirt and donned his jacket, glancing down at Lily, who was still staring nervously at the welcome party outside.

'I suggest you prepare yourself and remember what I told you. Because, as you've realised, you're about to meet the Queen of Nabhan.'

And worse, he thought, running a hand through his hair in vexation as he headed for the exit, much worse than that, they were both about to encounter the force of nature that was his mother.

# CHAPTER FOUR

LILY TUGGED NERVOUSLY at Khaled's oversized shirt. Was she really about to be introduced to a queen? While dressed like a charity case herself?

She wrapped steadying fingers around the handrail and stepped from the plane straight into a wall of heat. A pool of sweat bloomed in the small of her back.

Khaled, looking annoyingly cool, had reached his mother and bent to kiss her cheek. Even as he straightened, Lily saw the other woman watching her approach.

Dressed in a lilac linen dress, with a matching jacket draped casually about her shoulders, the Queen was even more beautiful in person than in her photographs.

The marriage of England's 'It' girl, Eleanor Wallace, to the widowed King of Nabhan had been the romance of the age. She'd been eighteen, he twelve years her senior, when they'd been introduced and fallen head over heels in love. Her family had objected to the match, arguing she was too young to take on the role of consort to a foreign king…too young to be stepmother to his three-year-old son.

Eleanor hadn't agreed.

Within two months they'd been wed. Ten months

later little Faisal had gained a half-brother with the arrival of Khaled. Three decades on and she'd made an art form of bending people to her will.

Such was the nature of the creature awaiting Lily has she arrived at Khaled's side.

'Mother, allow me to introduce Lily Marchant. Lily, this is Her Majesty the Queen of Nabhan, my mother.'

'Please, call me Eleanor,' she said, raising Lily up from her curtsy. 'And there's no need for that, my dear. We're not big on ceremony here. I'm only sorry it's taken you so long to visit us. The girls in particular will be thrilled to meet you.'

'Nate suggested they holiday together in Nabhan,' Khaled explained. 'As he couldn't join her straight away I offered to bring Lily with me, so she wouldn't have to travel alone.'

'That was thoughtful of you, darling,' Eleanor said, watching Khaled's bags being carried from the plane.

Lily's were conspicuous by their absence.

'Miss Marchant's luggage has met with an accident,' he said. 'Her hotel had a problem with its sprinkler system.'

'How unfortunate.' Eleanor glanced at the plasters on Lily's shin. It was obvious she didn't believe the story.

'Mother…' Khaled's eyes were grey flint '… I hadn't expected to see you this morning.'

'I found myself with a few spare hours.' She

flashed him a dazzling smile. 'So I thought it would be a nice surprise if I came to meet you.'

Khaled remained unmoved. 'I see. And the cars I requested?'

'Oh, I sent them away, dear. I presumed you would be coming to the palace with your guest.'

A muscle ticked in Khaled's jaw. 'Miss Marchant won't be staying at the palace. I've offered her and Nate the use of the waterfront penthouse. One of the cars was to take her there.'

'At the new harbour development? What a lovely idea. It's so close to the old city and it makes a wonderful base to explore from. You'll love it there, Miss Marchant.'

At that, Khaled appeared to relax.

Which was the moment Eleanor made her move, stepping between them and taking Lily's arm.

'But I won't hear of you staying alone while you wait for your stepbrother,' she said, leading her away.

Lily could almost taste the anger pouring off Khaled. They might have just met, but she decided she liked Eleanor already.

As they climbed into the limo Khaled moved to join them.

'No, darling,' said the Queen. 'You take the other car. You must have calls to make, and Lily and I will only disturb you with all our girl-talk. We'll see you back at the palace.'

Before he could protest, Eleanor's door had closed and the car was pulling away. Leaving her son standing on the Tarmac, entirely out manoeuvred.

Lily glanced back to see him, with an expression like thunder, stalking towards the remaining limo as the security team scattered to clamber into theirs.

'Oh, dear,' said Eleanor, with a mischievous glint in her eyes. 'Does he look much put out?'

Lily nodded.

'Well, it does a man good to be thwarted once in a while. Khaled is far too used to getting his own way. Though not with you, I think?' She sent Lily a disconcertingly knowing look. 'I doubt it was just my turning up unannounced that got him in such a temper.'

'Well, he's… We're…' Recalling Khaled's warning not to divulge any information, Lily fell silent.

'Don't worry. I won't pry,' Eleanor said, patting Lily's hand. 'But if he's been high-handed you mustn't let it bother you. Under that gruff exterior he's actually a kind and thoughtful man. He puts everyone else's comfort first. Everything he does is for his family and his country. Since his father's illness he's worked so hard…'

Eleanor's voice trailed away sadly.

There was truth, then, in the stories of Khaled's

punishing schedule since the King had suffered a series of heart attacks.

The cars had cleared the airport now, and joined a broad modern highway. Desert stretched away to far-off mountains in the west, and to the east was sparkling turquoise ocean. The motorcade sped north, towards the modern glass towers and the redbrick old town of Nabhan City.

Eleanor chatted…pointing out landmarks, putting Lily at her ease.

They'd reached the bustling suburbs. Men in long white robes sat drinking coffee outside roadside cafés, while women in vibrant headscarves gossiped on street corners. A group of schoolchildren ran along the pavement, waving at the cars and their royal occupants. Lily even spied a camel sitting sedately in the rear of a flatbed truck, travelling south.

All around her lay a new landscape, far removed from the sleepy green countryside she'd grown up in, and despite her worries for Nate she felt excitement ripple through her.

'It's beautiful, isn't it?' Eleanor said. 'I still remember how I felt the first time I encountered all this. We arrived late afternoon and came along this very road. The sun was setting beyond the mountains. I'd never seen anything so affecting.' She gave a wistful sigh. 'There's something about Nabhan that gets under one's skin. Of course, it helps that the men here are as sexy as hell.'

She chuckled at Lily's startled expression.

'Forgive me. I was remembering how Khaled's father looked, sitting right where you are now. Bassam was quite something… But then you've seen the son. I'm sure you can imagine.'

Again there was that penetrating look.

Lily turned away to hide her blush. Yes, the son was spectacular—but she'd rather not dwell on that, or the physical effect he seemed to be having on her.

Their car slowed and passed through gates flanked by saluting soldiers. The motorcade swept past them and up a wide drive, climbing through an avenue of soaring date palms. Then came the palace. Built of pale rose sandstone, the sprawling two storey Family Wing and the adjoining Royal Court buildings still managed to convey the sense of a family home.

Lily felt welcome the moment she set foot inside the cool entrance hall. A grand curved staircase led to a first-floor landing, while beneath her feet the white marble floor shone like glass, with a perfect reflection of the high domed ceiling above and the vast chandelier that hung there.

'Khaled's grandfather built the palace and he was fond of putting on a show,' Eleanor said, following the direction of Lily's gaze. 'But this hallway is rather beautiful. I know I'm truly home when I step into it.'

Lily stared in awe.

'What did you expect, Miss Marchant?' a deep voice drawled behind her. 'Tents? Huts built of earth?'

Khaled's car had arrived. Unfortunately his mood hadn't improved during the journey.

'Of course not,' she retorted. 'Nate has told me how beautiful your home is, but his descriptions haven't come close to the real thing.'

'Khaled!'

A delighted yell came from the top of the stairs as a blur of denim-clad coltish limbs and streaming ebony hair slid down the banister and launched itself at him.

'Amal, *habiba*.' He caught the slender girl and placed a kiss to the top of her head. 'Have you been good while I've been away? How are your studies progressing?'

Amal groaned. 'Why do you never ask about anything interesting—like, maybe, who's coming to Daddy's anniversary party?'

Then Amal saw Lily, and her eyes widened in surprise.

Khaled disentangled himself and set his sister in front of him. 'Please forgive the informal arrival, Miss Marchant, and allow me to introduce Amal—one of my baby sisters.'

Amal rolled her eyes. 'We're fourteen—and I'm the elder by ten minutes.'

On the landing above, a second figure appeared.

'Hanan, get down here!' Amal said in an excited stage whisper. 'Khaled's brought an actual girl home.'

Eleanor muffled an un-regal snort behind her hand.

Her brother scolded Amal for her unseemly behaviour.

It didn't dampen the twins' excitement.

After giving her big brother a hug, Hanan asked, blushing, 'Are you Nate's Lily?'

Ah… It looked as if her stepbrother had a young admirer.

Khaled called both girls to his side, producing a book for each from his pocket. He drew their attention to something he'd marked on one, and three dark heads bent over the pages.

'Since they were babies, whenever he returns from a trip Khaled always has something for the girls,' Eleanor said.

Memories of her stepbrother's homecomings came to mind. He was the only person who'd ever been pleased to see her, seeking her out the moment he arrived and gathering her up in a bear hug.

Where was he now? Lily's throat tightened. Moisture prickled behind her eyes.

At that moment Khaled's gaze lifted to hers. Now he was surrounded by his family, the grey flint had melted into a beguiling tenderness. It reached out, embracing her, too, soothing her moment of distress.

He held her gaze and the air became thick.

Time slowed.

The twins, his mother, the staff around them… all faded to shadows hovering at the edge of a dream.

She saw only him.

The glint of the chandelier lights in his ebony hair. The high slash of his cheekbones. The firm, full lips and that molten silver gaze, pinning her to the spot.

A strange yearning tugged at her womb and his nostrils flared like a big predator, catching her scent. On a broken breath Lily's hand fluttered upwards and settled across her heart. She didn't know if it was a defensive gesture or a way to control its wild pounding.

Khaled's brow knotted. Away went the tenderness, back came the flint.

'Mother,' he said sharply, 'Lily is tired. Perhaps she could be shown to whatever guest room I'm sure you've organised? Now, if you'll excuse me, I have work to attend to.'

'Of course. But, darling, you've been travelling all night, and I know you won't have rested. Won't you take a little time off and join us for coffee?'

'No, I'm afraid I can't.'

Eleanor sighed sadly as she watched her son disappear along the corridor linking the Family

Wing to the Royal Court, while Lily wondered what had just happened. One minute he'd been chatting with his family, and the next it had been as if that burning look had consumed everything around them and they were the only two creatures left on the planet…

'We love our big brother to bits, Miss March-ant,' Amal said, 'but I think we should warn you he can be a totally grumpy workaholic.'

Lily attempted an answering smile.

'You do look tired, my dear,' Eleanor said. 'Why don't we show you to your rooms, where you can rest?'

The twins led the way up the staircase to a ve-randa with ornate metal balconies. In the court-yard below there were lush plantings and fountains tumbling into tiled pools. Lily even caught the chattering of birds as they swooped between the trees.

'They used to keep caged songbirds here, but Bassam had them released,' said Eleanor. 'They must have liked it here, because they stayed.'

Lily was enchanted by it all. 'It's beautiful.'

'You should see it at night, when the lanterns are lit,' Hanan said, with a stunning smile.

She shared her brother's fine-boned features, and it was only a small step to imagine how he might look, should he choose to smile at her, too.

That brief heated look notwithstanding, since walking into his suite last night he'd been nothing but stern. Ever the Sad Prince, even here, in the heart of his family. Weighed down with cares, perhaps, or still tortured by the tragedy that had changed the course of his life.

Lily's heart softened at the memory of the teenage boy she'd first known. She could only guess at the responsibilities heaped upon the man now.

'I think you'll enjoy this suite.'

His mother had paused at a set of doors. Lily swiftly untangled her thoughts.

'It's the most comfortable we have, and the views are wonderful,' Eleanor said, ushering Lily into a stunning set of rooms.

Cream sofas scattered with silk cushions and side tables of intricately carved rosewood sat before arched windows that led to a balcony with a view of the sea. To her right, in a second room, a vast bed stood dressed in ivory linen, piled with downy pillows.

Eleanor placed a hand to Lily's cheek. 'We'll leave you so that you can rest. A servant will come later, to help you find your way around, but for now take as long as you need.'

She gathered up her girls, and in a flurry of goodbyes they were gone.

Lily took a breath.

It would be too easy to be seduced by all this. Eleanor had been so kind, and the twins had obviously been excited to meet her.

And then there was the Crown Prince himself, and the impact of that searing look.

Not ready to explore the reasons for that, she explored her suite instead.

The bedroom alone would swallow her entire flat back home.

Another floor length window led to the balcony. Lily pushed it open and stepped outside.

Eleanor hadn't exaggerated. The views were beautiful. Below there were more lavish gardens, and beyond a cluster of sand dunes and a beach of ivory sand that ran down to the sea.

Lily inhaled a breath of clean salt air laced with the warm spicy scent she'd noticed when she'd first stepped from the plane. Was even the air itself seductive in Nabhan?

A yawn erupted from somewhere.

How little sleep she'd had in the last few weeks since her stepfather's death, with the hurried sale and clearing of the house. Was it really less than a day since she'd deposited her possessions in her new shared flat? Mere hours since she'd hidden in Khaled's dressing room?

It wouldn't hurt to rest a little. Then, later, she'd figure out how to help Nate.

She lay down on the bed, sank into blissful comfort and, lulled by the distant wash of waves on the shore, closed her eyes.

Her last thoughts were of a sad teenage boy

who'd become a sad beautiful man. A man with a haunted expression but such gentle hands.

Mercifully, before she could torture herself further, Lily was asleep.

Lily woke with a start, confused by the unfamiliar surroundings and the lingering images of a dream she hadn't had in years.

She'd dreamt of Khaled.

Not the man he was now, but the grieving sixteen-year-old she'd first met that summer in her stepfather's house.

She'd been nearly eight, and would have proudly shared that fact with anyone interested enough to ask. No one ever had.

But one day that summer the household had been even more uninterested than usual, with the staff in a complete flurry. A school friend of her stepbrother had arrived suddenly and mysteriously, and nobody would answer her questions except to say he was 'Prince Khaled' and not to be disturbed.

'A prince?' she'd asked breathlessly. 'Like in Cinderella?'

'Never you mind,' they'd said.

She hadn't minded. Quite the opposite. She'd been thrilled that there was someone in the house even remotely close to her own age. None of her friends lived nearby. Nate was away on a school expedition. Her mother kept to her rooms. Even her stepfather, who mostly ignored her anyway, was abroad on business.

But more than that, there was a real, live *prince* in her house.

There'd been a man seated by the library door. With his deeply tanned skin and bald head he'd seemed rather intimidating, but then he'd smiled, said his name was Rais, and asked if she'd come to meet her guest.

Amazed that someone thought her important enough to meet the visitor, she'd forgotten to be nervous and nodded.

'Well, then,' he'd said, opening the door for her, 'you'd better go in.'

The room had been flooded with sunlight. Dust motes from ancient books danced in the beams that hit the floor. It had taken a moment for her eyes to adjust, to see the tall figure standing in the shadows beyond the window.

He'd been dressed in a black suit and tie. A neatly folded handkerchief had peeked from his breast pocket. A man's attire, though he'd really been still a boy. His dark hair, cut short at the sides, had been luxuriant on top and tumbled over his forehead. Thick ebony brows had sat above deep-set eyes of a startling pale grey. His long straight nose and chiselled cheekbones had lent him an aristocratic air.

He had been the handsome young prince from any of her favourite fairy tales come stunningly to life, and quite simply the most beautiful thing she'd ever seen. Right there, Lily had lost her heart.

She'd drawn nearer and greeted him.

As he'd swung towards her his expression had shocked her and, being so young, and unused to company, she'd said the first thing that came to mind. 'Why are you so sad?'

The teenager, wrestling with a raw grief he'd hardly been able to comprehend, had replied just as honestly. 'Because my brother died.'

The moment the words had left his mouth he'd been overcome. She'd instinctively wanted to help this boy, and had gone to clasp his hand in her own. She had remembered the one thing that her own stepbrother loved, and had used it to try to divert him.

'Do you like horses?'

The Prince, too distressed to speak, had given a nod.

'Nate has three. We could go and see them if you'd like?'

He hadn't known how brave she was being even to mention them. They terrified her. Her father had died when he'd been thrown from his horse.

'Yes,' he'd said. His grip had tightened on her hand as if clutching a lifeline. 'I'd like that a lot...'

Lily sat up and swung her legs over the side of the bed.

No, that bewildered boy was nothing like the

man he'd become. He was not even like the man who, six years later, had been so kind to her at her mother's funeral—who'd found her sobbing in a cloakroom, pulled her close and allowed her to weep all over him.

The man now was harder, colder. More remote.

So how—when she recognised that, and when life had taught her to rely only on herself—had she let that moment in the hallway blur the edges? Imagined being in his arms again while he fended off the world and all its pain for her.

The man had a kingdom to rule, and an entire people to protect. What time would he have for the likes of her?

Through the window, she saw the sky was almost dark. She'd slept all day. She'd been more exhausted than she'd realised. Not only last night, but the preceding weeks had taken their toll.

In the sitting room a servant was moving about. As promised, the Queen had sent someone to help their new guest.

A bath had been drawn, and when Lily emerged fresh clothing had been laid out. The embroidered linen tunic and slim trousers were comfortable and cool, even matching Stella's sandals. Her damp hair was dried and styled to fall in burnished curls down her back.

'His Highness asked that you be brought to him once you had risen,' the servant said.

Bathed and dressed, ready to be taken to the Prince?

Lily's heart thumped with an entirely inappropriate anticipation as she was led through airy corridors and quadrangles open to the skies where the verdant green of clipped box softened stark slate pools.

They'd left the Family Wing and entered the Royal Court—a large complex with all the private offices, public reception rooms and staff areas required for a modern working royal family. Staff hurried past, intent on their evening duties. They bowed to Lily, politely concealing their curiosity. Mostly.

Several times she caught looks that lingered longer than necessary. Perhaps their prince bringing home 'an actual girl' was a surprise to the palace staff, too. They couldn't know that it was the intervention of his mother that had brought her here…that her son had intended she be secreted away from public view and from him.

She refused to feel a moment's disappointment about that.

Up ahead stood a pair of imposing doors, flanked by two of the palace security team. Across the threshold waited Rais and a sumptuous salon. Stately gilt-edged sofas and chairs were arranged around the perimeter. A vast Persian rug covered the floor. And on the walls hung a series of elaborately framed mirrors.

This must be Khaled's *majlis,* or public reception room.

As Rais showed her to a seat she considered who else had visited here. Prime ministers, presidents, other royals… Since Khaled had taken on his father's role, probably all of them.

From beyond a second set of doors the murmur of voices reached her. One had a deliciously deep rumble. The voices grew louder as the doors opened. She took a deep breath. She must remember she was here for Nate. There was nothing delicious about it.

Then Khaled walked in and every good intention deserted her. Dressed head to toe in black, his hair tousled as if he'd just run a hand through it, he was utterly, bone-meltingly beautiful.

He crossed the floor in a few easy strides. 'Lily, I trust you are rested and feeling refreshed?'

'I am, thank you.'

She sounded breathless. She was. That face. That *voice.*

She shifted position, sitting back on the sofa—only to find her feet dangling in mid-air. She quickly tipped her sandals off. They landed on the carpet with a soft plop as she folded her legs beneath her.

A royal brow lifted. Perhaps it was inappropriate to be so casual in these surroundings, but right now she didn't care. She couldn't let him see how he'd affected her just by crossing a room with his elegant, loose-limbed stride.

It didn't help that she knew exactly how he looked beneath his clothes. Only a narrow stretch of body between waist and thigh was a mystery. Her gaze lingered there before she looked away, horrified that she was actually mentally undressing the man.

Khaled settled in the seat opposite. 'Your room is satisfactory?'

'Yes, thank you. The suite is lovely.' Being angry at her situation was one thing—being ungracious quite another. And at least he was trying to be civil. 'The view from the balcony is fabulous.'

Khaled looked puzzled. 'The view?'

'The gardens and the beach?'

His eyes narrowed. 'You are in the guest suite in the Family Wing?'

'Your mother said it was the most comfortable.'

'She's correct, it is. But those rooms are reserved for particular friends of the family—which, under the circumstances, I'm sure you would agree you're not.'

So the polite veneer hadn't lasted long. Gone, too, were all traces of the passionate interlude from that morning. The Stern Prince was definitely back.

She lifted her chin. 'Should I ask to be moved, then?'

'No, it would cause too many awkward questions. You will have to remain there for the time being.'

'And how long will that be? You can't just keep me here. I have a life to start in London. A new flat…a job.'

'I understood you were unemployed at present.'

He wasn't asking a question. It was a statement of fact. She'd been lying about the job and he knew it.

'For what it's worth, I'm sorry—at least for that part of your predicament.'

She was surprised to hear genuine compassion.

'I'm not completely heartless, Lily.'

'All evidence to the contrary…'

His jaw tightened. 'You break into my rooms, search my possessions, and you accuse me of behaving badly?'

'I wouldn't have been there at all if you hadn't believed the worst of someone you should trust. Nate isn't capable of betraying you.'

'And you,' he said sharply, 'are fooling yourself. He's left you alone to deal with this. You are only here because of his dishonesty.'

'No. I am only here because he had to ask me for help. He should have been able to come to you, his oldest friend. But you've sunk so low as to abandon him.'

Khaled's face hardened. 'Let me make things perfectly clear for you. You are here because I want it and you will stay here as long as I wish. As you have pointed out, your stepbrother and I are old friends, and for that reason alone I haven't yet involved the authorities. But one way or another Nate will be caught. Until then you will be staying in Nabhan, and while you are here you will obey me.'

'Obey you?' Lily shot to her feet. 'I will not. You have no power over me.'

She headed for the exit, determined to leave, only to find an apologetic but nevertheless unmoving Rais in her way.

'As you see,' that annoyingly cool voice said from behind her, 'you will remain here until I decide you may leave—and that includes right now. Sit down.'

By the door stood a marble-topped table bearing a small bronze of a Roman warrior. His lips were pulled back in a snarl and his arm was raised, brandishing a lethal-looking sword, ready to mete out damage to anyone in his way. Had it not been so finely wrought, and probably valuable, Lily might have scooped it up and launched it at Khaled's pompous head.

But, having no choice she returned to her seat, dropping into it as petulant as a scolded teenager.

Khaled calmly brushed an invisible speck from his trousers. 'My family are expecting us to join them for dinner. They believe you're here to explore Nabhan with your stepbrother. I've told them

Nate has been delayed on charity business but will be joining you soon. Remember, they also think you arrived without luggage because it was ruined when the sprinkler system malfunctioned at your hotel.'

'You mother didn't believe that nonsense for a second.'

A muscle ticked in his jaw. 'Then it's your job to convince her it's true.'

'I won't do it.' She sprang from her seat again, faced him with her hands fisted at her hips. '*You* invented that ridiculous story. *You* convince her it's true.'

She stalked away to wait at the door. It would have been a most satisfying finale to their conversation had she not forgotten her sandals.

Khaled rose from his seat and bent to gather them up. He strolled over to her, placing them in her hands. 'At least they're a better fit than the shoes you tried to steal from me.'

She stared ahead, ignoring his jibe.

He caught her chin in his hand, turning her face to him. 'I will remind you, Lily, of the precarious position you are in, and I absolutely will not allow you to upset my family or compromise my integrity in any way.'

Despising herself for the way his touch sent shivers through her, she snapped back. 'You should have thought of that before you kidnapped me.'

She was gratified to see a flicker of alarm in the depths of those clear, grey eyes.

He released her. 'There is still the option to involve the authorities,' he said, his voice silky and menacing. 'We have police cells in Nabhan every bit as accommodating as those in England. I suggest you keep that in mind.'

And he nodded for Rais to open the door and let them pass.

# CHAPTER FIVE

'GOOD MORNING,' SAID the solitary occupant of the breakfast room. 'You must be Miss Marchant.'

Lily had been directed here by a servant. She'd hoped to find the twins or the Queen. Even the King himself. They'd made feel her welcome last night. Unlike the scowling, monosyllabic Prince, who'd brooded in a corner for pretty much the duration of the evening.

There'd been no repeat of that heated moment in the hall yesterday, and she'd almost convinced herself she'd imagined the whole thing.

'Forgive me,' the stranger said, smiling, 'but as the family is elsewhere I'm obliged to introduce myself. I hope you will excuse the lapse in manners?'

His manners appeared to be as impeccable as the immaculate grey *dishdasha* and white head-covering he wore.

'I'm George Hyde-Wallace,' he said, inclining his head, 'cousin to the Queen and her children and Leader of the Council of Families.'

Lily knew of him. Who didn't? The passionate Arabist who, four decades ago, had settled in the region, embraced all things Nabhani and risen to the top of its society. Weather-beaten, sinewy and straight-backed, there was a restless energy about him that belied his seventy-four years.

'I'm delighted to meet the person who has so captivated the twins. They would talk of nothing else this morning.'

He smiled again, though it didn't quite reach his eyes. Instead they were watchful, assessing. Lily had the curious feeling that George Hyde-Wallace had been waiting for her.

She offered a restrained smile of her own. 'I'm pleased to meet you.' She stretched out her hand. Did she imagine the pause before he took it? Perhaps, because now he'd clasped it firmly in both his own.

She glanced at the coffee cup and newspaper next to his seat. 'I was told I might find the family here. I'm sorry if I disturbed you.'

Dark eyes swept her from head to toe. 'Think nothing of it. If only all interruptions were as charming. But I regret the family have already breakfasted. However, I am here.' He squeezed her fingers once before letting go at last. 'And I am failing in my duty as stand-in host. Have you eaten? Please…' he indicated the seat next to his '…join me.'

He called the servant, ordered breakfast for her, then waited politely for Lily to sit before seating himself.

'I understand you are here to explore Nabhan. Have you decided where you'll begin?'

Of course not. As Khaled had so graphically informed her, this was no holiday. How did she answer?

'I'm fascinated by the country's history.'

'Excellent. Well, we have extraordinary treasures here. Dating back millennia. And, conveniently, I happen to know the Minister of Antiquities. I'd be happy to organise a private tour of our National Museum.'

George's gaze was intense. His attentions equally so. Lily was grateful for the jug of fruit juice that arrived at that moment. She busied herself with pouring a glass.

'Once your stepbrother has arrived, of course,' he said. 'Is he expected soon? The family seemed a little vague on the matter.'

His expression was bland. The question felt anything but.

'I think so. Nate heads off around the world so often it's hard to keep up.' She hoped she sounded convincing.

'Ah, yes. The intrepid Nathaniel Marchant.'

For 'intrepid' she could infer any number of insults, judging by the man's tone.

'It's a shame he's not here with you,' he continued. 'Of course in the meantime you have the protection of the Crown Prince himself.'

And what on earth did that mean?

She was saved from this increasingly disconcerting conversation as a breakfast tray was set down beside her.

*'Bon appétit,'* George said, smiling, and returned to his newspaper, leaving her to eat in peace.

The tray held a paprika-spiced omelette, served with plump tomatoes. There were diminutive chapattis, the size of her palm, and an engraved silver pot of sweet, cardamom-scented tea.

She'd taken her last sip when a servant approached. Khaled wished to speak with her.

She glanced at her companion, about to make her apologies, but he was already on his feet.

'Don't worry about me, my dear Miss Marchant. You must not keep His Highness waiting. I'm sure we'll see each other again soon. In fact I'll make sure of it. But for now, goodbye.'

This morning there was no waiting in the *majlis*. Lily was taken directly into Khaled's private office.

He was behind his desk, on the phone, speaking in Arabic. He glanced at her, nodded once, then continued his conversation.

It was left to his aide to offer a more polite welcome. 'His Highness will be a moment, Miss Marchant. I am Sabir, his secretary. May I bring you some refreshments while you wait?'

Lily declined, but for this man who had at least shown some manners she offered up her best smile. Blushing, Sabir departed to his own workstation in an anteroom.

Khaled's frowning gaze watched his secretary's hasty retreat, then swung back to her, glaring, as if she'd deliberately discomfited his staff.

She stared right back, one brow raised, until he returned to his call.

Free to look about her now, Lily was surprised to see none of the grandeur of the *majlis*. The room was merely businesslike. She would have expected something that spoke of Khaled's status, but apart from a long, leather sofa and a sideboard set back against the wall, there was only an austere wooden desk and two chairs facing it, one of which she occupied.

No antique furniture, no fancy artwork—barely any individual touches at all except for a framed picture on his desk. She couldn't see the subject. His parents, perhaps? His sisters? Or…she bit her lip at the comical idea…a favourite horse?

By far the most striking feature of the room was the wall behind Khaled's desk. Lined from floor to ceiling with books. Hundreds of them. In English, Arabic, French, and on every imaginable subject. A cursory glance took in volumes on history, economics, engineering. There were political biographies and classical works from ancient Greek and Roman authors, and those were just the English titles she understood. All his? She was awed by the hours of reading those shelves represented and the fierce intellect of their owner.

Tucked away at the far end of the last shelf, and quite different from the rest, sat a small group of slim leather bound volumes. She peered closer, trying to make out their titles, but became aware of a sudden stillness from the figure on the other side of the desk.

Khaled was listening to his caller, but she knew from his frown that the look of censure was meant for her. What? Was she supposed to stare meekly at her feet until he deigned to speak to her?

He swivelled his chair away, laying his free hand flat along the desktop as he continued his conversation. The sleeves of his close-fitting white shirt were rolled up, revealing muscled forearms covered in fine dark hair. The solid links of the gold watch clasped about his wrist enhanced the lean strength of his hands. Strong hands that she knew could be so gentle.

Lily absently twirled a lock of her hair, remembering how he'd tended to the cuts on her leg. Remembering the warmth of his palm wrapped about her calf, the glide of his fingers as they secured the bandages to her shin. What if he'd gone higher? Over her knee…along her thigh—?

'Good morning.'

She jumped. The phone call had ended while she'd been busy fantasising about him. Furious with herself—she didn't even *like* him—she lifted her chin and offered a frosty, 'Hello.'

His expression was equally cool. 'I'm returning some of the possessions you lost the other night,' he said, beckoning to Sabir.

On the desk, the secretary placed the beaded evening clutch that she'd last seen hurtling into the rose bed beneath Khaled's balcony. Remarkably, it looked none the worse for its adventure. No scuffs, no dirt. She opened it. No phone or anything else of real use either.

'If you were wondering, you've had no messages or calls from your stepbrother,' Khaled told her. 'Neither has he responded to any we've tried to send or make to him.'

'I was supposed to message him when I left the party. He'll have worked out I'm with you. He won't get in touch. He'll know you'll try to trace him. But I should call my flatmates. They'll be worried.'

'They've already been reassured that you're safe. They were most impressed that you're a guest of the Nabhani royal family.'

'They wouldn't be if they knew the truth,' she muttered, rummaging through the remaining contents of the bag.

Her wallet was still there, though her bankcards were missing. All that was left was the folded tote she'd planned to use for Nate's laptop, an expired train ticket, and the money she'd kept for her taxi home the evening of the charity event.

No phone. No cards and a pitiful amount of cash.

Khaled wasn't taking any chances.

'I was wondering what you will do when you return to England?'

She glanced up. The question had thrown her.

'Look for work,' she said. 'I need to support myself as soon as possible.'

'I see. Perhaps it's a little indelicate to ask, but how much money do you have?'

'Enough savings to cover two months' rent and living expenses. Three if I'm careful.' Where was he going with this?

'Three months? That's all?'

He sounded appalled. It wasn't her fault she hadn't been able to save much. Edward Marchant's fortunes had been ailing for years—so, too, had the allowance he'd begrudgingly paid her.

'And after that?'

'I guess I'm on the street if I don't find a job,' she replied tartly. How was this any of his business?

'What about the provision your parents made for you in their wills? They both had personal wealth.'

'Whatever money there was, my mother signed over to Edward Marchant.'

'All of it?'

'My dad left everything to my mum. I guess he thought she'd take care of me.'

His snort told her what he thought of that decision. 'So your mother's poor judgement means your inheritance is lost?'

He seemed so angry. A secret, silly part of her was thrilled that he might be genuinely concerned for her. Who'd ever cared enough to get angry on her behalf before?

'Like your stepbrother's.'

Okay, not concern. Accusation.

She swallowed down her disappointment. 'So now I'm guilty, too, because I need money?'

'No, I think you've been duped. Nate's laptop has been thoroughly checked. There's nothing on it to prove his innocence. In fact, quite the opposite. It proves he personally transferred ten million pounds from the charity funds into a private account.'

'Ten *million*?'

Khaled stared at her. 'I gather he didn't share that detail with you. It's about the same sum his father squandered. Perhaps your stepbrother was simply replacing his lost inheritance.'

'You can't honestly believe Nate would do something so out of character—and for money? He'd never expected to have an inheritance, and he didn't want it. He wanted to make his own way. You know he and his father didn't get on.'

'Yet all the evidence points to him. He disappeared at exactly the same time as the money.'

'But you've been friends for years. Is that really the man you know?' She fixed him with an expectant look. 'What does your gut tell you? Do you really, truly believe Nate could steal anything?'

That tell-tale muscle ticked in his jaw as he gazed back at her. Then he exhaled heavily, as if a deep tension had left him. 'It is, as you say, out of character.'

She scooted to the edge of her seat. 'So, what are we going to do about it?'

He raised a brow. '"We"?'

'You think I'd sit and do nothing when Nate needs help?'

She jumped up and began to pace. She didn't see his gaze follow her, darkening as the morning sun gilded her hair into a curtain of fire.

'It's about his schedule. Did someone hack into his diary? They seemed to know exactly where he'd be. You said the theft happened while Nate was using his bathroom.'

'I said nothing of the kind.'

She waved a hand vaguely in his direction. 'Must have been Nate who told me that.'

'Did he, now? What else did he tell you?' He sounded suspicious again.

She turned on him. 'For heaven's sake. You've just admitted it can't be him, so start looking for other solutions. Think of a way to help him.'

He didn't answer. Instead that intense grey gaze studied her. As if sizing her up. She forced herself not to look away, even though an annoying heat began spreading across her cheeks.

'Actually,' he said eventually, 'there is a way you can help.'

Lily let out a breath. 'Excellent. What can I do?'

He stood and ambled round his desk towards her. 'If Nate truly is innocent, the longer we can keep the theft quiet the more time we'll have to find out who really did it. So we need a distraction. A smokescreen, if you will. That's something you can help provide.'

He'd stopped a pace in front of her. Close enough for her to truly appreciate the breadth of his muscled chest under that snug white shirt.

She forced her gaze back up to his face. 'I... I can?'

'Yes. And we must also consider that my mother's showy greeting at the airport and your presence in the palace means that people will have certain expectations.'

She frowned. 'What expectations?'

'That I have serious intentions about you.'

'Isn't that a bit over the top? This isn't Regency England.'

'No, it's Nabhan, and it's a proud Islamic nation. Modest and conservative. Society here is very traditional. As Crown Prince I must, of course, be seen to respect those traditions.'

'And what does that mean, exactly?'

'It means we get engaged.'

Holy…*what*? She couldn't have been more shocked if he'd suggested she strip naked and do cartwheels through the palace.

'How would…?' She swallowed, hard. 'How would our being engaged help Nate?'

'Think about it. If the real culprit is attempting to ruin your stepbrother, or to drive a wedge into our friendship, proclaiming you as my future consort and him my future brother-in-law would show they have failed.'

He'd spoken at least two full sentences, but Lily's attention snagged on only one word.

*Consort.*

Said in that sexy rumble of his, it started a reel of X-rated images playing through her imagination. It didn't help that he was standing so close. The heat of his body made her fingers flex, as if they wanted to splay out across his torso and get toasty in all that warmth.

She scrunched them into fists at her sides. 'Why would anyone believe you've chosen me, a nobody, when you've had your pick of countless high-profile women? You've famously left a trail of broken hearts all over the globe.'

A brow rose at her less than flattering description of him. 'Because you are unlike anyone I have been associated with before. A well-born girl of limited experience.'

'Limited—'

'A virgin.'

Lily gaped at him. 'That's a big assumption to make. Anyway…' she folded her arms across her breasts '…you're wrong.'

*Liar.*

She'd never trusted anyone enough to do *that* with them. Everyone in her past who should have loved her had let her down. She wouldn't risk being hurt again. She only trusted herself now.

His eyes had followed her defensive move. 'I see. You have some experience. Then what's making you so nervous?'

'I'm… I'm not.'

'But I only have to look here…' He laid two fingers across the pulse beating furiously at the base of her neck, then lightly brushed the line of her collarbone to the hollow at the base of her throat. 'You have a very revealing blush.'

She swayed towards him, snared by those grey eyes.

Then, all matter-of-fact, he lifted his fingers clear. 'You do know it wouldn't be real?'

Her gaze refocused. 'No—I mean, yes…of course.' She clumsily tucked a lock of hair behind her ear. 'I know that.'

'And we don't actually have to make an announcement. A suggestion that we're serious will be enough.'

She pulled herself together. 'Who else will know it's a pretence?'

'Apart from us? My father, Rais and Sabir.'

No mention of the Queen.

'You'd lie to your mother about this?'

'If we want a quiet life, yes. If she knows we're pretending she'll do everything she can to make it real. The moment she heard you were on that plane my mother began concocting romantic plans for us. I assume you understand they are her plans? Not mine.'

She didn't want there to be any plans either. So that was good. Wasn't it?

'However, I have asked her to take you shopping, to buy you a new wardrobe for your stay.'

'You organised all that before consulting me? I don't want it. I buy my own clothes, and right now I'm fine.'

His gaze swept her linen tunic and trousers. 'No, you're not. It would be inappropriate for my prospective fiancée to be parading around in borrowed clothes...' he glanced at her feet '...and stolen shoes?'

She was still wearing Stella's sandals. 'They're also *borrowed*,' she reminded him, 'and I can't afford to buy new clothes.'

He looked at her as if she was an idiot. Of course he would be paying for them.

'I'm looking for Lily. Is she with my son?' Eleanor's voice floated in from the anteroom.

'Right,' Khaled murmured, 'time to practise looking like you're madly in love with me.'

'I'm mad, all right,' she answered, just as Eleanor walked in.

Khaled hesitated just long enough before jumping away from her, to appear as if they'd been caught embracing. Lily glowered at him.

'I'm sorry if I'm interrupting.' The Queen didn't look sorry. She looked thrilled that there might have been something to interrupt. 'I'm here to take Lily shopping, as instructed, but I can come back later if you're in the middle of something?'

'Only your son being a tyrant again,' Lily muttered.

He shot her a quelling glance.

In a grey sheath dress, Eleanor looked elegant and cool. The exact opposite of how Lily was feeling. How had this man got her so worked up so quickly?

She had to fight back. 'I'll manage with some T-shirts and a skirt or two.'

Perfectly adequate for a fake fiancée.

'My dear, fashion is my one vice,' Eleanor said. 'Allow me the fun of helping you chose a wardrobe for your stay.'

'By the way, I've decided to join you,' Khaled announced, ignoring Sabir's startled expression. 'Whatever was planned for this morning can be rearranged.'

Eleanor's eyes danced. 'But, my heart, you despise shopping.'

'Not at all—in fact, it will be a pleasure.'

From where Sabir stood, frantically reviewing the diary, came an incredulous snort which, too late, he tried to disguise as a cough. Horrified by this dreadful slip in etiquette, he made his apologies and fled to the anteroom.

Eleanor was leaving, but as Lily followed her arm was caught and Khaled bent low to speak in her ear.

'Remember, you'll be dignified and restrained, as would befit my fiancée, and you'll curb your insolence while you're with my mother.'

'It won't be hard to be nice around Eleanor. I actually like her.'

'Then that should make it easier for you to convince her we're serious about each other.'

'How I am supposed to do that? I can hardly bear to look at you.'

They'd reached the cars. Not limos today, but a line of four-by-fours.

'Improvise,' he said sweetly, placing a hand on her back and giving her a shove towards his mother's car.

'Oh, don't you start,' she muttered, dredging up a smile and walking towards the Queen. 'Nate said that, too, and look where it got me.'

# CHAPTER SIX

HIS MOTHER WAS RIGHT. He did loathe shopping. But her interference yesterday had forced a change of plan. This was him regrouping and turning events to his advantage.

The Qaydari King was dragging his feet on the terms Khaled wanted. He'd lay odds on the man changing stance when a potential new bride appeared on the scene.

As for the missing charity funds, he admitted Lily might be right about her stepbrother's innocence. Resolve that issue, too, and she could return home. An outcome he'd have been fine with until that revelation about how little stood between her and destitution.

He'd been appalled to discover she was so vulnerable, and had dealt with it in the only way available to him: by getting angry. Of course it was none of his concern, but somehow the moment he'd hauled Lily on that plane she'd become his…his…

*His.*

No, damn it, not that. Never that.

What he meant was his *responsibility.*

That moment in the hall yesterday had meant nothing. The sight of her tear-filled eyes had moved him—that was all.

The ache in his groin almost made a liar of him, but he knew that for what it was: abstinence. He'd been celibate since beginning negotiations for his marriage. It had nothing to do with the specific female now on the other side of the dressing room curtain.

So what if she'd been interestingly flustered earlier, which had made him wonder, despite her claims, if any man had touched her? His blood had leapt at the thought, but he'd quickly mastered that. All that should concern him was ramping up the rumour mill. If his plans worked there'd be a rash of photos across the media in the next few hours. The sole purpose of his presence here.

In the meantime, he resigned himself to a dull hour or two of shopping. Provided he made some appreciative noises here and there, his contribution would barely be needed.

He picked up a newspaper from the pile laid out for him and applied himself to the first article of interest.

Ten minutes later the curtains swished back.

He politely lifted his head.

And all the air left his body in one breath.

An actual physical punch to the gut couldn't have had more impact.

The sea-green silk dress was simple enough: cowl-necked, cap-sleeved, cut to the knee. But it flowed in sinuous, loving lines over breast, hip, thigh. Despite the plaster and healing grazes to her shin, Lily looked…

With a flourish, Eleanor gathered up all that glorious auburn hair and caught it with a clasp at the nape of Lily's long pale neck.

*Beautiful.*

The assistant produced matching heels, urging Lily to slip them on. Now there was also the arch of an instep and taut, shapely calves to contend with.

Eleanor twirled her fingers in the air, encouraging Lily to execute a spin.

'Charming. Absolutely charming.' She turned to Khaled. 'Don't you agree, darling?'

Where, he thought, slightly panicked, had those enticing curves come from? She'd felt almost girl-like when he'd lifted her aboard the plane.

'Indeed,' he muttered, mourning the loss of the linen tunic and Stella's flat sandals.

Lily was studying her reflection in the mirrors, as if she couldn't quite believe the transformation a simple dress had achieved.

She wasn't the only one.

He was still staring when the curtain closed again.

Then a clothes rail was wheeled into the room and left beside him.

Khaled exhaled slowly.

Lingerie. Lots of it. In a heart-stopping selection of silk and lace, and in every colour from virginal white to sex siren's scarlet.

Somewhere a door opened, and a gust of air dislodged a pink lace thong from its hanger. Downwards it went, to land close to his left foot. It lay there, delicate, distracting, an utterly feminine contrast to the robust dark tan leather of his shoe.

He slid his foot away, resumed his reading.

But the pale pink lace refused to be ignored.

Khaled's gaze drifted from the newspaper.

Creamy seed pearls had been stitched in a heart shape across the lace at the front. A bow graced the back, designed to sit just above the swell of a shapely bottom. But it was all so insubstantial it would fit easily in his closed fist.

His fingers tightened, feeling not the newspaper but the softness of lace, the pearly nub of a lustrous bead.

From beside him came a soft cough. An assistant had returned to the rail and, her lips pressed tight together, was watching him.

A grown man. Infamously stern. Leader of his people.

Transfixed by a silly scrap of lace.

He made a great show of adjusting his newspaper, and to his relief the rail, plus offending panties, disappeared behind the curtain.

Unfortunately the respite lasted only moments.

'You must try this pink lace bustier,' he heard the assistant say. 'It gives a wonderful shape. And there's a matching thong. The bows and pearls are so pretty. It's a popular set for honeymoons.' There was a conspiratorial chuckle. 'I'm told it brings bridegrooms to their knees.'

The newspaper was forgotten.

Concealed by nothing more than a fall of fabric, Lily and those curves were feet away, trying on man-slaying lingerie.

A message arrived on his phone from Rais.

They're here.

Thank God. He wasn't sure how much more of this he could take.

He typed his response.

Expect us in five minutes.

Time to action the next part of his plan.

He dumped the newspaper, banished all thoughts of Lily in pink lace, and beckoned an assistant over.

'I'd like to see the green dress again. With the heels. Her hair up. Neater this time. Maybe a little make-up.'

The assistant disappeared behind the curtain to deliver his instructions. He heard a murmured discussion, one voice louder and increasingly indignant. But the Crown Prince had asked and, no matter what the objections, those assistants would deliver exactly what he wanted.

Minutes later the curtain was drawn back to reveal their handiwork: Lily in the green dress and heels. Glaring at him, hands fisted at her hips.

'Well, do I come up to scratch?'

*Perfectly.*

Except for the angry stance and mutinous look. They wouldn't suit his purposes at all. It was time to bring back the softly flustered woman from earlier.

Khaled stood and began strolling towards her.

Lily watched as Khaled came closer, all smouldering masculine intent. Seconds ago she'd been in a snit. Now she couldn't remember why. By the time he reached her she was boneless and unresisting, letting him gather her hand and lift it to his lips.

'*Habiba*, you are beautiful,' he purred.

Beautiful? Her breath fluttered out. Dear Lord, she'd sighed. She'd actually just sighed.

He dipped his head. He was going to kiss her. She shivered as warm lips brushed the tender skin of her ear. A delicious, scintillating caress.

But not a kiss.

He was whispering to her.

'Something has come up. Follow my lead.' Louder, for the benefit of the others, he said,

'Mother, ladies, our apologies. An urgent matter needs our attention and we must go.'

Okay. It was part of the act.

'Can I leave you to gather everything Miss Marchant will need for her stay? You have her sizes?' The assistants nodded vigorously. 'And please send a selection of everything you think appropriate.' He turned to gaze adoringly at her. 'Don't stint.'

As if they would. They were staring at him as if he were a god come down to earth, imagining all their commission.

His long fingers curled through hers, warm, strong and wonderfully comforting—drat the man. And then he set off for the private lift they'd arrived in.

*Focus, Lily.*

He'd said something had come up. Perhaps there was news on Nate?

The lift doors closed. 'What's so…?' Where had that husky note come from? She tried again. 'What's so urgent that we needed to leave?'

'This.' He gathered her close and pressed his mouth to hers.

She should have pushed him away—there was no audience here—but his mouth slanted over hers in a kiss so tantalisingly gentle she leant in. He began a delicate exploration of her jaw, her throat, and found a tender spot beneath her ear, teasing it with a slow swirl of his tongue.

Her fingers sank into his biceps.

When he nudged a thigh between her legs she instinctively rubbed against it, seeking contact where she needed it most.

'Come,' he said.

*Yes, oh, yes...*

Wait...no. What?

He was walking. He meant she should go with him. He was leaving the lift.

She teetered in her new heels and he drew her protectively against his side. Together, eyes locked, they crossed the foyer and stepped outside into the now familiar intense heat and something else—something new.

With the dazzle of sunshine came camera flashes. A cacophony of voices. Crowding figures.

'Your Highness? Sir? When's the wedding?'

'Lily? Has he bought you a ring yet? When did you know it was love?'

She blinked as the lights exploded, over and over. With a jolt she realised he'd walked them into a press pack—and he knew enough about those for it not to be an accident.

Beside her Khaled purred his answer, poised, prepared. 'I have no comment at this time,' he said, guiding her towards a waiting limo, its door held open by Rais.

A limo? What had happened to the four-by-fours they'd arrived in? And the security team that materialised around them had doubled in size from earlier.

He'd set the whole thing up. They even had her name.

She came to her senses as fury replaced all that melting distraction.

She'd been played.

If he thought he could whisper a compliment, ply her with kisses and she'd go just along with this charade, he was in for a shock.

She swivelled in Khaled's arms and aimed herself at the nearest reporter. 'Actually, I'm sorry to say there won't be an announcement any time soon.' Every microphone strained towards her. 'His Highness is a great believer in tradition, so I know he would never propose without formally asking permission of my stepbrother.'

'And where is he, ma'am? Will he be arriving soon?''

'He's so busy I have trouble keeping up with his timetable. But, Your Highness…' Lily batted her eyelashes at him '…he's your most loyal friend. I'm sure you'll know where Nate is.'

All faces turned eagerly in Khaled's direction.

The little madam. She'd pay for that.

'He'll be joining us soon,' he said, propelling her forward in earnest now. Time to get her into the car before she did any more damage.

She was halfway in when some buffoon shouted, 'Are you going to say yes, Lily?'

Her head popped up. Tempting as it was to manhandle her back in, he knew it would make too much of a scene. He was forced to grant her the last word.

'I'm not sure. There's wealth and status in his favour, but I've also been reliably informed that he's a bit of a grumpy workaholic. So, you know, guys, it's gonna be a tough decision…'

*Hell.*

To the sound of laughter and a barrage of new questions Khaled bundled her onto the back seat and climbed in after her. She scooted to the far side, folded her arms, then stuck her nose in the air, all puffed up like an indignant chicken. If he hadn't been so angry he might have laughed.

'Congratulations. Far from keeping Nate under the radar, you've now encouraged every reporter from here to Buenos Aires to hunt him down.'

'Perhaps if you'd told me what to say before you walked me into *that*—' she flung a hand back in the direction of the dispersing journalists '—I might have reacted differently.'

'All you had to do was walk beside me and pretend you're in love. Why was that so difficult? I also said "dignified and restrained". Are you forgetting our agreement already?'

'Funny, that. You say agreement… I say blackmail. But what's a small semantic difference between friends? Anyway, you told me to improvise, so I did. And while we're on the subject of that little farce, don't ever kiss me like that again.'

'I was also improvising. I needed your compliance. It seemed the quickest way to get it,' he said, settling back and stretching out his legs.

He saw her gaze flicker over them, lingering where his flexed thigh strained against the fabric of his trousers. He waited until her eyes lifted back to his. He raised a brow. She flushed at being caught ogling, but her nose went higher.

'Well, don't do it again. I didn't like it.'

He did laugh at that bald lie. 'Yes, you did. A man doesn't…what was it?…break hearts all over the globe without knowing when he's pleasing a woman.'

Awareness flared in her eyes, as if she were imagining how he might please her again, but her mouth compressed into an angry line.

'I doubt you'd know how to please a woman if you were presented with detailed diagrams and precise written instructions.'

'Really?' he said, oddly insulted. 'Care to test that theory?'

The instant she uttered that stupid remark Lily knew she'd made a mistake. Khaled loomed closer, grasping her chin, his stormy gaze fixed on her mouth.

She pushed at his chest. 'I don't think we—'

He kissed her.

Whatever words she'd been about to say, even the thought that had prompted them, disintegrated under the hot, hard press of his mouth. The entrancing gentleness was gone. Now there was just heat and anger.

She knew he was punishing her disobedience, but her traitorous body didn't care. It craved more of him…his kisses, his touch. It wanted to be *pleased*.

A big hand spanned her ribcage, pulling her close. When his thumb brushed the sensitive underside of her breast Lily moaned and opened her mouth beneath his, inviting him to feast.

He accepted the offer.

With a growl, he hauled her onto his lap, his hands roaming free. One drifted down her thigh, over her knee, then retraced its path. The hem of her silk dress was riding up with the steady glide of his fingers. Then they disappeared beneath the fabric altogether and slid between her thighs.

His touch was incendiary. Building the heated throb of desire that had started the night he'd brought her here. She whimpered, restless and edgy, and shamelessly spread her legs wider for him.

When a finger slipped inside her knickers, to slide into the wet heat between her legs, he muffled her gasp with a kiss, his tongue exploring her mouth with the same stunning intimacy his fingers were employing elsewhere.

Now his lips went to her neck, his nose brushing along her jaw to that sweet spot behind her ear, and Lily's head fell back.

Her world shrank to this: Khaled's cheek against her hair, his deep voice murmuring hot, delicious demands—'Yes, let go…show me…'—and the wicked rhythm of his fingers.

Her body answered his every demand, reacting in ways she'd never known it could, climbing higher and higher. Almost overwhelmed, Lily clamped an arm about his neck, hovering taut, suspended.

'Please…' she begged, mindless with need, not truly knowing what it was she pleaded for.

Until he pressed his thumb against her…just so.

'Come for me,' he ordered—and, oh, God, her body obeyed him, shattering in panting, moaning ecstasy. She sobbed into his shoulder, clinging to him, riding out an orgasm so intense only the anchor of his solid bulk kept her from flying into pieces.

Slowly she came to, her heart rate slowed and her breath steadied. Khaled traced soothing circles across her spine and murmured to her in Arabic. As though all his English had deserted him.

Lily lifted her head and warily met his gaze. The grey eyes glinted with a strange emotion that looked incredibly like wonder. She sighed as he pressed a kiss to her lips, so sweetly tender it reached into all the lonely, abandoned places in her soul.

Like the day all those years ago when, her mother gone, she'd hidden in that cloakroom so alone and lost. He'd spoken to her in Arabic then, too. Held her as she cried. Been there for her when she'd needed him.

What pleasure had he taken just now? None. It had all been about her. *Her* pleasure, *her* needs.

Those empty spaces that craved love and belonging, that she'd thought permanently sealed up, had been filled with warmth and, more dangerous still, hope.

The world turned and Lily trembled, nearly believing…

On a whoosh of air, the car door opened. Out on the palace forecourt the servant looked astonished to find the Prince's guest not in her own seat, but draped all over the Prince himself.

And with crashing hurt she remembered.

This wasn't real.

That tender kiss, that dazzled look. They were lies. Like the rest of it. All done to gain the thing he wanted. Her compliance.

She unclenched her fingers, dismayed to find she'd crushed one side of his collar and torn two shirt buttons loose. There was even a small bite mark in the curve where his neck and shoulder met.

Khaled was speaking to her, stroking her, trying to reassure her, but she batted his hands away, scrambling from his lap to land in an undignified heap at the feet of the startled servant.

Before he could help her up she'd shot to her feet and raced up the steps into the palace, about to bolt for her rooms. But they'd arrived at an unfamiliar entrance and she had no idea which direction to take.

Those few seconds of indecision allowed Khaled to catch up. His arms went round her. She tried to squirm free.

'*Habiba*, shh… It's all right.'

But she felt too damn used to be calmed by him. 'I don't want you touching me.'

He flinched. 'You were telling me something different in the car.'

'And you took full advantage of that, didn't you?'

Her cheeks burned in humiliation, but he was right. Even now her whole body hummed from being held by him. She shoved at him, trying to escape. She might as well have tried to move a mountain. He'd braced every muscle to hold her still.

'Behave. You're supposed to want me in public. Not just when we're alone together. So you're going to take my hand and trot along beside me like the adoring girlfriend I need you to be.'

She glared up at him, but read the warning in

those grey eyes. She'd do as she was told if she wanted to help her stepbrother.

*Nate*, she thought, offering up her hand, hating the sizzle of energy as Khaled's fingers closed around it, *what's happening to me?*

The staff they met gaped at him as he strode by, hand in hand with a woman. With her flushed cheeks, swollen lips, she looked ravished, undone. Khaled gritted his teeth, hating that they could see her like this.

*Mine*, a possessive voice nagged him. *Not for their appreciation.*

Sabir greeted them as they crossed the threshold of his office. 'Good afternoon, Your Highness, Miss Marchant. I see the shopping trip was successful. Your dress is most becoming.'

'Thanks, Sabir. His Highness chose it,' said Lily, sending Khaled a filthy look. 'Then he had me dolled up and paraded in front of the press.'

'Yes, the…ah…the pictures are circulating already. Excuse me, Miss Marchant, but His Highness has a call waiting. Sir, you'll want to take this straight away.'

Lily tugged her hand free, quickly moving from him to stand at the window, her arms wrapped about her waist. The protective gesture nipped at his conscience.

Not taking his eyes off her Khaled reached for the receiver. 'Azir.'

Expecting to hear the Qaydari ambassador, requesting an urgent meeting, he was stunned when instead came an entirely different but deeply familiar voice.

'Is that the grumpy workaholic? This is your loyal friend speaking.'

Khaled spun away from Lily to hide his shock at hearing Nate Marchant.

'You've got a nerve, ringing like this,' he said, switching to Arabic. Nate had travelled extensively in the Middle East and was fluent. 'Where are you—and where the hell is the charity money?'

'How should I know? I didn't take it.'

'Then why does all the evidence point to you?'

'Because someone went to a lot of trouble to set me up. But never mind that now. I'm checking on Lily. Is she with you in the palace? Is she okay?'

Khaled glanced at her. 'Yes.'

It was an honest enough answer to the first question. The accurate response to the second was up for debate. She looked vulnerable and brittle and lost.

She swung round to face him. 'You're busy,' she said, 'and I'd like to freshen up.'

'No, wait.' He couldn't let her go like that.

But she'd whisked out of his reach. Though she paused at the door. 'The flowers are a nice touch, by the way.' She gestured at a bowl of roses on his desk. 'They soften you up a bit—and, let's be honest, you could do with it.'

The blooms had appeared during their visit to the store. Most certainly placed there by order of his mother and precisely for that reason, no doubt. But he didn't need softening up. He just needed people to do what they were told. Not elaborate or interfere. Or damn well improvise at the wrong moments.

'What was that about flowers?' Nate asked. 'Hang on, was that Lily?'

'Yeah.'

'Out of your depth already?'

Khaled bristled. 'Certainly not.'

He was the Crown Prince. He'd been de facto King for seven years, shouldering the responsibility of the entire nation. Little fazed him now, and certainly not a mere slip of a girl. He was not, nor ever would be, out of his depth.

'So if you've been set up who's behind it?'

'You have to ask? He hates that we're friends. He hates your reforms. He's engineered a way to get rid of me and discredit you at the same time.'

'Impossible. He wouldn't dare.'

'Yes, he would. Discredit you and you'll lose the support of the Council. He'll put a stop to every one of your reforms. You're telling me you really hadn't considered it?'

Khaled dropped to the sofa. 'The implications are so bad I didn't want to face it.'

'If the theft becomes public and you can't get any evidence against him you'll have to. Parading

Lily around as your girlfriend is genius, though,' Nate continued. 'Even if news gets out, who's going care? It'll buy us some time.'

'That was the idea,' Khaled said.

'She's agreed to it all?'

He ran a hand across his brow. 'She isn't being as obliging as I'd hoped.'

Nate chuckled. 'Yeah, I saw the footage outside the store. By the way, how did you catch her in the first place?'

'My rooms. She climbed the ivy and broke in via the balcony.'

Nate whistled. 'That's a ballsy move. And you expect a girl like that to meekly trot after you, pretending she's in love?'

She hadn't been so averse to him in the car.

The roses caught his eye. His mother wanted a great romance for him. Most decidedly he didn't. It would get in the way. But did that mean there couldn't be passion? He wondered if the Qaydari Princess would be as thrillingly responsive as Lily had. He pushed that thought aside. That wasn't important. Their union wasn't about his pleasure.

'Sabir,' he called, 'take these flowers away.'

'I'll put them on my desk, sir.'

'You will not. You'll stick them somewhere out in the corridor, where my mother can see them. The same with any more she tries to put in here. For whatever reason.'

'Of course, sir. No flowers. Under any circumstance.'

Nate's disembodied voice came again, sounding amused. 'Having a tantrum over a few flowers? Like I said, mate, you're out of your depth.'

'Where the hell *are* you?' Khaled snapped, irritated by the other man's enjoyment.

'Doesn't matter right now. I have friends doing some digging. I'll get back to you. Keep Lily safe, won't you? Until we know exactly what's going on.'

'Of course. Isn't that why you sent her on that wild goose chase in the first place? So I'd bring her here?'

'She'd have been determined to help in some way otherwise, so that's what I hoped you do once I'd realised you thought I'd stolen from you. What the hell, mate? What was going on in your head?'

Khaled grimaced, feeling guilty for the first time. 'In my defence, if someone has set you up, they've made a damn good job of it.'

'*If?*' Nate shouted, and cut the connection.

Khaled tossed the phone aside. Why did the Marchants think they could ride roughshod over him?

He crossed to the window where Lily had been. His fingers drifted to the sore spot on his neck. If her claim to be experienced was true he had a low opinion of her lovers. Whoever they were, they'd obviously been selfish bastards, seeing to their own pleasure and ignoring hers. Because that had been the first time a man had given her an orgasm. He'd bet his life on it.

Was that why she'd looked so shocked? As if the world had just shifted beneath her feet and she had no idea how to deal with it?

He wanted to do it again—but next time he wanted them both naked and to be buried to the hilt inside her when she came apart.

He ran his palm down his face.

There would be no repeat. It would only complicate matters.

He put it from his mind.

He had more important things to worry about.

Back in her sitting room, Lily was feeling just as conflicted. Thinking she was either about to burst into tears or sprint from her room, run towards the beach and never stop. She just couldn't quash the idea that something momentous had happened.

Which was ridiculous.

All she'd done was make out with a man in the back of a car. People did that sort of thing all the time.

Except in this case the man was a prince, the car a bulletproof limo, and it had felt like so much more than just making out. More as if she'd handed over an essential part of herself.

Why had she let Khaled touch her like that?

When she knew everything he'd done that morning had been to manipulate her? He'd said so himself. He was simply gaining her 'compliance'. Not only had she fallen for it—she'd practically flung herself at him.

She started moving, heading for the bathroom. She had to get back to being in control, safe. She'd start by getting out of this silk dress. It rode up far too easily beneath a man's fingers…

She unzipped it and shoved it from her shoulders. She snatched up a face cloth and scrubbed at the make-up they'd applied at the store. Dragged the pins from her hair and yanked the style loose.

Then she saw her reflection in the bathroom mirror.

Wild eyes, swollen lips, hair tumbling in disarray about her naked shoulders. Who *was* this wanton?

Through the fall of her hair she glimpsed her bed, and conjured an image of Khaled lying there. Naked. Stretched out over her. Deep inside her.

Lily snapped her thighs together. That was never going to happen. She wouldn't allow it.

She turned her back to the mirror. Not wanting to see that woman any more. Not wanting to be her.

Her hands were shaking as she finished stripping everything off, including her tell-tale damp knickers. Those she shoved straight into the laundry bin, slamming down the lid on the evidence of what she'd been doing.

She'd come apart in Khaled's arms. So overwhelmed by her body's reaction she'd bitten his neck. Her eyes squeezed shut against the excoriating embarrassment and the shameless thought that quickly followed.

Could another man deliver her to such abandon?

Lily sank her face into her hands as an ancient feminine instinct whispered back. *No, just him. Always and for ever, just him.*

In the shower, she cranked the water to scalding hot and scrubbed at her skin, washing away the feel of his hands, the scent of his skin, attempting to expunge every trace of him.

When her skin was pink and her fingertips shrivelled to walnuts she gave up, dried herself and tugged on a bathrobe. The black lace knickers she'd arrived in that first night, now freshly laundered, were tucked away in a drawer. She pulled them on. They might only be simple lacy pants, but they were from her regular life, and right now they felt as substantial as armour.

And what of Nate in all this? Pretending to be Khaled's girlfriend was all about helping her stepbrother. To help him, would she steel herself to do it?

Yes.

But there'd be no more kissing or touching. And

absolutely no repeat of the incident in the car. She'd resist, whatever Khaled did.

There was a knock at the door.

The knot of excitement in her belly wasn't a good start. But surely it wouldn't be him.

Out on the veranda stood Eleanor. Behind her was a seamstress and three palace maids, each with a dress rail loaded with boxes and garment bags bearing the department store logo.

'Khaled said you'd come to lie down for a while. If you're still tired we can come back later, but all the goodies from the store have arrived.' Eleanor smiled hopefully. 'I thought you might like an afternoon of trying things on.'

Some retail therapy? The perfect diversion.

'Actually…' Lily reached for the Queen and practically dragged her in. 'Now is great.'

# CHAPTER SEVEN

AFTER CHECKING IN with his mother, and hearing that Lily had spent the afternoon happily trying on everything that had been delivered from the store, Khaled felt his earlier unease dissipate.

She had looked, Eleanor told him, 'stunning', 'gorgeous', and 'perfect'. When she'd added, in rapturous tones, that she'd been the very image of a modern princess, he'd decided it was time to change the subject. Lying to his mother about Lily's presence in Nabhan was necessary. He'd no desire to completely rub her nose in it.

Keeping away from Lily this evening seemed expedient, too. 'I won't be there at dinner,' he'd told his mother. 'I have work to do.'

Always. He made sure of it.

For once Eleanor hadn't tried to dissuade him. Instead, she'd sent in the big guns.

The King had walked into his rooms just after dark, asking why his son wouldn't be joining them, brushing aside Khaled's protests and declaring that if the Crown Prince failed to take at least occasional time off he'd also be having heart attacks.

He'd slapped his son jovially on the back, but Khaled had seen the flicker of pain in his father's eyes. It never sat well with the King that he could shoulder so few of his responsibilities, and that his son was being forced to deal with them in his stead.

If it eased his father's sense of guilt, he'd give up a few hours. Guilt, Khaled understood. It was the thing that drove him.

Now, an hour after everyone else, he climbed the stairs to the rooftop restaurant. He saw her at once. Standing alone at the edge of the terrace, looking out over of the old city. The hem of her dress fluttered in the evening breeze. Her hair fell in loose waves down her back.

She looked like a girl, he thought, with an ache in his chest, and yet not. She was a woman, and everything they'd done in the car that afternoon only confirmed it.

No matter. There'd be no repeat of that.

Something caught her eye in the street below and she smiled a sweet, sad smile.

The ache deepened.

Then, on the other side of the terrace, unaware of Khaled's arrival, a man rose to his feet, his gaze fixed on Lily.

George Hyde-Wallace.

It took seconds. And done before he even knew he meant to do it. But suddenly Khaled was at her side and the other man was sinking back down, forgotten, into the shadows.

When Eleanor had said they'd be dining at a favourite restaurant in the old city, Lily had expected some grand establishment. Not this magical roof garden dotted with brass lanterns, where the royal party reclined on rugs and cushions, serving themselves from copper platters, with the restaurant owner and his family sitting amongst them and everyone gossiping like old friends.

Lily watched it all with a quiet, bittersweet delight. So this was how it felt to have family…to belong.

Her gaze roamed again over the cluster of groups. Only one man was missing.

Khaled had been noticeable by his absence when the whole family—even George and an off-duty Rais—had piled into the fleet of cars waiting on the palace forecourt. She'd chided herself for the stab of disappointment. After today's incidents, surely the less she saw of him the better.

Needing a moment to herself, she'd risen from the cushions and moved to the edge of the terrace. In the street below a couple emerged from one of the homes. Their tiny daughter, her hands clasped safely in theirs, toddled between them. With a wistful smile Lily watched the doting parents guide the little girl safely across the street.

Had there'd ever been a moment when her parents had walked with her like that? Keeping her safe…the centre of their lives?

'My father claims that from this restaurant you can see the four corners of the world.'

Lily whirled round at the sound of Khaled's voice.

He stood a few paces away.

'It's a bold statement,' he continued, 'but I think he means the four corners of Nabhan. To him, of course, it's all the same thing.'

He was watching her with a warmth and intensity that rendered her quite speechless.

He stepped closer.

'Let me show you.' He stretched out his arm beside her shoulder, pointing to the open plain beyond the edge of the suburbs. 'To the north you can see the beginnings of the marshlands.' The moon had risen and its gleam was reflected in a distant patchwork of streams and tidal flats. 'It's recently been designated a conservation area. It has a rare and sadly endangered collection of flora and fauna. In fact, I've just launched a charity to support it…'

The corner of his mouth lifted in the ghost of a smile, and she knew he was teasing her. She'd come apart in his arms this afternoon and she'd vowed not to let him under her defences her again. But how was she supposed to resist this charm?

His hands settled on her shoulders. He turned her so she looked over the heads of the gathered party and across the flat rooftops of the old city to the harbour and the ocean beyond. That simple contact raced through her body. To places she'd really rather it didn't.

She focused hard on the view before her. In the marina the lights of luxury yachts and pleasure cruisers sparkled, while out at sea giant tankers rode at anchor.

'For centuries merchants sent their ships from here, loaded with frankincense and pearls and purebred Arabian horses,' he said. 'They went east to India and China. The trade made the city wealthy. Now those tankers provide a different source of wealth. No less vital to our people, but perhaps not as romantic.'

The sultry evening breeze, laden with the scent of spice and the salt tang of the ocean, tugged lightly at her dress. From a terrace nearby came the strains of a slow, sweet melody.

He turned her again, and the gap between them closed. She felt the solid wall of his chest against her back. 'And to the south?' she asked breathlessly.

'To the south is the Rub' al Khali…the Empty Quarter. Nothing for hundreds of miles but sand dunes, scorpions and the occasional Bedouin tribe. It's beautiful, but one of the harshest places on earth.'

She barely heard the words, conscious of his breath ruffling the top of her hair, of the heat of his body so close to her own. She fought to hide the way he was affecting her.

As he turned her again his hands slid down her arms in a light caress. She kept her own hands curled tightly by her sides. At least they had their backs to his family now.

He bent his head, his mouth level with her ear. 'Do you see that line of shadow on the horizon?'

Citrus and spice and that certain indefinable something that was just him swirled around her. She closed her eyes and breathed him in.

'Yes,' she whispered, in truth seeing nothing at all.

Every sensitive nerve-ending along her cheek and neck tingled with awareness. As if some elemental charge pulsed back and forth between them. She turned her head, her eyes flickering open, and Khaled met her gaze. The soft light had turned his grey eyes black, picked out all the haunting curves and lines of his face.

He was breathtaking.

Her lips parted and his gaze went unerringly there. His head dipped, angled as if he meant to kiss her. She tilted her face upwards.

From one of the groups behind them came a flurry of laughter. Abruptly Khaled released her. With a sharp intake of breath he stepped back.

'That dark line on the western horizon is the foothills of the Sakhr mountain range.' His voice had hardened. 'A ridge of almost impassable granite and schist that separates us from Qaydar, our nearest neighbour.'

Why had his expression become so desolate?

'I can see why your father makes his claim,' she

said, smiling up at him, wanting to bring back his earlier teasing.

But there was no answering warmth. The shutters had slammed down.

He was staring at the mountains. The moonlight picked out forbidding summits and deep, fathomless wadis.

'I actually came over to talk to you about something else,' he said, his expression as distant as those far-off peaks. 'What you told me this morning has deeply concerned me. I had no idea you had so few resources to fall back on. I'd like to help you, if you'd permit me?'

'Thank you, but I'll manage by myself. I always have. I actually prefer it that way,' she said. Their stilted politeness felt so weird after what he'd done to her in the car this afternoon.

'Of course. I remember you look after yourself. You were adamant about that once.' There was that ghost of a smile again. 'But perhaps on this occasion you might accept the assistance of a friend who is concerned for you? If it helps, consider it a favour returned.'

Oh, how tempting to accept, to lean on him, to have all his strength in her corner…

'But I think you've already repaid that particular debt,' she said. 'You helped me once, too, remember?'

He inclined his head in agreement.

One of the staff approached with a tray of coffee and dates. For two.

Khaled glanced at his family, who all appeared to be deliberately looking anywhere but in his direction. With a sigh, he indicated the cushions nearby. The servant left the tray on a low table beside them and he waited for Lily to sink down, folding her feet beneath her, before pouring and offering her a cup.

Her fingers trembled as she took it. The acerbic Khaled, she realised, wasn't anywhere near as intimidating as the stern, quiet man opposite her now. Tonight, the male diners were all in traditional Nabhani dress, so perhaps it was the fault of the grey *dishdasha* he wore, the twist of the snowy white *ghutrah* about his head.

But he looked only slightly more stunning in traditional robes than in formal black tie. It was the man, and not the clothes that was so arresting.

'I presume you have so little money because you worked for your stepfather?' he asked. 'He couldn't pay you?'

Wrestling with the emotions unleashed by the last few minutes, Lily didn't reply at once, keeping her eyes fixed on the expanse of rug between them.

'Forgive me,' he added, 'perhaps I'm being impertinent?'

She shook her head. 'No, you're not. It's a valid question. The answer is no, not for the last few months. And it was never that much when he did pay me.'

'Then it puzzles me…what was it that kept you in that house once you were old enough to leave?'

She looked up at him. 'Because it was my home. At least the only one I've known. And it suited my purpose to stay. I studied at the local college and it was cheaper to live there than to move out.'

'But your stepfather insisted you work for him as a condition of your remaining there?'

'As housekeeper, you mean? Yes, but it didn't really feel like work. I loved that house,' she said. 'The old library, my mother's roses. Even the leaky roof and the crazy antique plumbing. Yes, sometimes things were difficult, and I often worried over how we'd get the house through another winter without money for repairs. But I got to see Nate when he came home for visits, and Edward had been my guardian and the only parent I ever had. I guess I hoped that one day he'd—' She stopped, shook her head. 'You don't want to hear about this.'

'Yes, I do.' He reached out, taking her hand in his. 'Tell me, please.'

She looked at their entwined fingers, then met his earnest gaze. 'I secretly hoped that one day he'd be like a real dad,' she said. 'You know…that he'd choose me first.'

'Choose you first?' he repeated, in a soul-steal-ing voice, and those little tendrils of hope came flooding back, curling around her heart.

'Everyone who should have loved me and looked out for me,' she whispered, 'they chose something else instead. My dad chose his career over his wife and daughter. My grandfather chose family pride over me. My mum… Well, you know how that turned out.'

She hadn't meant to share all that with him. But under that intense gaze and the slow caress of his thumb across her knuckles it had slipped out.

'So that's why you stayed with your stepfather?'

'Yes—though it made no difference. Edward couldn't have cared less. About me or my mum. Like my real father, I suppose. There's only one thing I know about him for certain. At the beginning at least, he loved Mum enough to defy my grandfather, make everything legal and get married. He must have cared then. I've clung to that.'

'Sir?' An aide had appeared and bent to whisper in Khaled's ear.

He listened, frowning. Then, with only a curt nod to her, as if she'd being talking about nothing more significant than the weather, he followed the aide from the terrace.

'That's the thing about royals,' said George, strolling over. 'One never really has their full attention. Aisha will understand, of course. Being royal herself.'

'Aisha?' Lily parroted, still stunned by the way Khaled had simply left.

'It's actually a secret. But I don't want to see you getting hurt, so I think you should know.' He sank to the cushions beside her. 'Khaled is in negotiations for the hand in marriage of the eldest daughter of the Qaydari King. Our border with them sits in the middle of the Sakhr mountains. I assume that's what His Highness was pointing out to you before?'

She'd poured out all that stuff about wanting someone to choose her first, stupidly thinking that Khaled genuinely cared. When what he actually cared about was the woman he was negotiating to marry—the woman he'd already chosen.

A stab of pain pierced her heart. Swift and sure. Lily didn't like the Queen's cousin, but she was grateful to him. He couldn't have told her about the Qaydari Princess at a better time. It reminded her that none of this was real. Khaled wouldn't ever really be there for her. Despite his offer to help.

Nothing had changed.

She was no worse off than before.

So why did it feel as though a piece of her had just split apart and fallen in two?

# CHAPTER EIGHT

THE NEXT MORNING the photos were everywhere.

Photos of her gazing up at Khaled, all dreamy and besotted as they stepped from that store.

Of him holding her hand at the restaurant while she looked helplessly dazzled.

*Pathetic.*

Lily flung her phone across the bed. She'd fallen for his false charm twice in one day and now there were stupid photos to prove it.

When she thought he'd steered them to a quiet corner of the roof terrace so they could talk privately, he'd been manoeuvring her to the best spot for the long-lens cameras.

Had that almost-kiss been part of the act, too?

She groaned and flung up an arm to cover her eyes.

Why did she have to think about that?

Because now she knew exactly what it was like to be kissed by him. The passion he could elicit from her body.

Her belly tightened at the thought. She flung up the other arm and blotted out the world completely.

So what if he was a great kisser and good with his hands? Okay, *really* good with his hands. How dense would she be to give her heart to the most unavailable man on the planet? Another in a line of people who wouldn't put her needs before his.

Didn't she know from bitter experience what that could do to a person?

Lily recalled other mornings when she was still very young, when she'd climb into her mother's bed and cuddle in close. Her mother would tell her stories about the amazing places she'd filmed in, the handsome men she'd acted with. *'Though none so handsome as your daddy,'* she'd say, with a sad catch to her voice.

Then she'd sit Lily at her dressing table, take up a beautiful ebony brush with silver inlays and gently tease the knots and tangles from her daughter's hair, the same dark red as her own. Singing to her—nonsense songs to make her laugh and distract her from any painful tugs, though she'd rarely hurt her. Her mother's fingers had been nimble and soothing.

But then had come the days when Mummy had been 'too tired', or wouldn't wake up at all, and there'd be a sour smell to the room and empty bottles on the bedside table.

After that Lily had learned to do her own hair. Raking at the tangles with a cheap plastic brush the housekeeper had bought for her.

Needing someone who didn't care had cursed her mother to a life of despair before leaving her only child to fend for herself.

But that child had survived and learned the lesson well.

It didn't matter how Khaled's touch made her feel. There'd be nothing but heartbreak with him.

Flinging open the wardrobes to rediscover her new clothes made her feel better. Forty-eight hours ago she'd had one good dress to her name. Now, cleaned and mended, it hung there, looking decidedly drab next to all its new and glamorous sisters. Everything from day dresses to the most exquisite but revealing evening gown that Lily doubted she'd ever have the courage or the right occasion to wear.

But today was a dress-down day. She was spending time with the twins later.

Rummaging through the rest of the selection Eleanor had insisted she keep, she unearthed a white cotton peasant blouse and denim shorts with cute turn-ups. Spying a colourful scarf on a shelf, she snatched that up, too, knotting it at her throat. She might feel miserable, but she was damn well going to look cheery.

Finally, after slipping on some wedge-heeled sandals and admiring her new look in the mirror, she decided that if she could find more of those chapattis and that scented tea they'd served her yesterday, she'd be about ready to face her day.

In the breakfast room, Khaled was taking his morning coffee. He was hidden away in a nook near the window, scrolling through the news on a tablet, when Lily strolled in.

His instinctive surge of delight was followed by irritation. It was barely past seven. He'd planned on being safely in his office long before anyone else was up. In particular Lily.

Yesterday's photos were circulating, and the press was filled with nothing but the Sad Prince and his new girlfriend, which meant the story was driving itself. There was really no need for him to see Lily while they were in the palace. Last night's accord could continue, while his people and Nate searched for the evidence that would implicate Hyde-Wallace.

So why was he gazing at her?

Right now she stood there, surveying the breakfast buffet. He noted the shorts. Obviously from the new wardrobe the Queen had helped her acquire yesterday. A scarf was tied at her throat. Accessories, too? His mother had been thorough.

Khaled was still for a long moment. God, but she looked young. Young and fresh and heart-stoppingly pretty. Her hair was caught up loosely in a clasp that left tempting tendrils spilling over her shoulders. A man would only have to lift a hand and a single tug would set all those glorious locks tumbling free.

Khaled reached for his coffee, giving his fingers an alternative occupation. He took a sip as Lily stretched to gather an apple from the fruit bowl. Her blouse rode up, exposing a slender midriff of smooth ivory skin. His fingers tightened as he remembered the petal-soft skin between her thighs...how she'd come apart when he touched her there.

The cup clattered back into its saucer.

This was intolerable. He'd been determined to put yesterday's events into their proper perspective. Not relive the more enticing moments. He'd allowed himself to be drawn in, to care what happened to her. When she'd whispered how she'd wanted Edward Marchant, that feckless social climber, to be a father to her, he'd reached for her hand without thinking...

It was probably as well that he'd been called away. He shuddered to think what he might have ended up saying to her. A woman could not be allowed to have this kind of hold over him. It was entirely unacceptable.

Sabir entered, on his way to his regular breakfast rendezvous with the Prince. Time to get on with work for the day. But his secretary halted as Lily greeted him and now, his morning duties apparently forgotten, he was retrieving his wallet to share photos of his baby daughter.

Lily's mouth spread into that bright, enchanting smile of hers and Khaled's heart constricted. What man wouldn't be stopped in his tracks by that?

Two days she'd been here.

*Two.*

Was that all it took for a man's self-control to begin slipping away? Well, not this man. The attraction was an aberration. He'd master it.

Rais walked in and joined the pair by the buffet. After a moment he threw back his head, guffawing at something Lily said.

Khaled's mood worsened. Since when did his grizzled security chief guffaw? First Sabir...now Rais. Was every one of his team under her spell?

His sisters bounded in.

'Lily! Mummy's going to invite you to stay until Daddy's anniversary party.'

'Say yes. Please.'

*No. Definitely not happening.*

He spoke. 'Lily.'

The flash of surprise in those big hazel eyes was followed by a wariness he thought they'd got past last night and which, to his annoyance, pained him. As he drew closer he saw she looked pale and drawn, as if she hadn't slept well. That troubled him, too.

Damn it, he was putting a stop to this nonsense right now.

'A word, please.'

He pulled her from her little fan club, marched her out into the corridor and backed her into a quiet alcove, using those precious seconds to wrestle his libido under control.

'It appears you're about to be issued with an

invitation to my father's anniversary party next month. You will decline.'

Lily shook free of his grasp. 'Can't you even say hello before you start ordering people about?'

'I didn't bring you out here to exchange pleasantries. We'll be ending our arrangement long before the party, and you will, of course, be returned home at once.'

Her expression brightened and she looked up at him with big, hopeful eyes. 'You think we're going to prove Nate's innocence soon?'

He'd barely given the man a moment's thought this morning, and now he was finding it hard to think at all while she gazed up at him like that.

'Perhaps. You'll need to be here for a few more days. You'll tell my mother you have a previous arrangement. A friend's engagement party, maybe.'

'How ironic.'

'And while you're here I'd prefer it if you didn't flirt with the staff. They have work to do, and you are creating too much of a distraction.'

For him, too. Right now it was those shorts and sandals. They were doing incredible things for her legs.

'Is that so?' she said, in a tone he didn't much care for. 'And here's me thinking I'm just being polite to people who have been kind to me.'

'That's not how it looked from where I was sitting.'

'You've been spying on me?'

He didn't answer that. He just stared down his nose at her. He didn't have to justify his behaviour to this woman. He was the Crown Prince. He did as he damn well pleased.

'Now I know why you've had to resort to black-mail to get a fiancée. You are absolutely without charm.'

Offended, he snapped back without thinking. 'I've had no shortage of women.'

'But a distinct lack of willing fiancées, apparently.'

'My previous partners had no interest in marriage to me.'

That had not come out the way he'd intended. And of course she instantly leapt on his mistake.

'Gosh, I can't imagine why…'

Now, quite frankly, her manner was insulting. No one dared speak to him this way. The tenuous grip on his temper began to slip. He planted a hand on the wall beside her head, shamelessly using the advantage of his height to tower over her.

'But, *habiba*,' he purred, 'I've had numerous thoroughly satisfied lovers.'

He was rewarded with that blush of hers, blooming over her neck and cheeks. But then she squared her shoulders.

'Good for you. I take it you went to their homes? It would be difficult bringing them here…

as you're still living with your parents. Does Aisha mind that, by the way? Your other potential fiancée.'

How the hell did she know that? He disregarded the jibe about him still living at home. He was not like other men. This was not a regular home.

'I have meetings this morning, but we'll discuss that later.'

She lifted her chin. 'I may not be available.'

'I'd advise on making yourself available.'

'Or what?' she challenged. 'What can you do without revealing that I'm only here because you've lost millions of pounds and have absolutely no idea where it is?'

'Perhaps your beloved stepbrother would enlighten us?' he sneered, ignoring the niggling voice of conscience that told him he hadn't let her know Nate was safe.

She rolled her eyes. 'How many times? He doesn't have it. Which you should have known from the start. I've had pet hamsters with more sense than you.'

She was comparing him to a *rodent*?

Nate was forgotten. With a growl, up went the other hand, trapping her between his outstretched arms. 'Don't taunt me. You won't like the consequences.'

She rose to her toes and pushed her face into his. 'I don't like it *now*.'

Hell, she was arousing. Her sweet rosebud

mouth was so close. He wanted to flatten her to the wall and ravish it until she melted against him.

'Sir?' Rais had emerged from the breakfast room.

'What?' Khaled snarled, not taking his eyes from Lily's.

'Perhaps you should take your conversation to a more suitable location?'

Yeah, his bed…with this woman sprawled naked beneath him, asking—no, *begging* for him to take her.

One of his sisters giggled. He dragged his gaze from Lily to see four people watching him: Rais disapproving, Sabir startled, and his sisters peering round their shoulders, looking gleeful.

Damn the palace and its lack of privacy—and damn the way this woman could rile him so easily.

He pushed away from the wall. 'This conversation is not over, and you will present yourself when sent for,' he said, spinning away, not giving Lily a chance to respond, and getting the hell out of there before he did something he might truly regret.

Sabir hurried after the Prince and Rais tactfully hustled the girls back into the breakfast room, leaving Lily alone. A small mercy.

She didn't know if she wanted to howl in mortification or pummel the wall in frustration.

Khaled was driving her crazy.

He'd crowded her—all hard, pumped-up Alpha male, trying to intimidate her. It had had the opposite effect. It had made her want to plaster herself against his chest, tell him to shut up and kiss her already.

This man who snapped at her one minute and the next looked as if he was about to ravish her. This man who was going to marry someone else.

*Oh, God.*

Lily buried her face in her hands. She didn't want to feel any of this.

'Madam?'

She snapped upright. One of the Queen's staff was hovering a few paces away.

'Excuse me but, if it is convenient, Her Majesty wonders if you will join her for coffee?'

Convenient? Jeez, this family's timing was something else. *Because here comes the invitation*, she thought. The one that she'd been ordered to decline.

With its ivory walls and carved rosewood shutters at the windows, the Queen's study was an oasis of calm after Lily's fraught start to the day. An elegant writing desk sat before a group of sumptuously upholstered sofas and armchairs, and on a low table in their midst, in a nod to the European origins of its owner, was a Wedgwood vase filled with blowsy English roses.

On a side table against one wall was a collection of framed photos—the kind of shots of family and friends to be found in the sitting room of any wife and mother.

Lily looked closer.

Although in this case the 'friends' were more likely to be found gracing the front pages of the morning newspapers or TV reports: they were famous faces in their own right.

What a potent reminder of how little she belonged in the Azir social circle.

Lily spun away—only to be confronted by the most arresting image of all.

On the opposite wall to the desk, in perfect view for whenever their mother raised her head, hung a large framed photo of the Queen's children.

It had been taken some years ago—the twins looked about six years old. They were on a tropical beach, the girls caught up in the arms of their big brother, each balanced on a hip. One brandished a prize for the camera: a great tangle of seaweed. The other was lost in a fit of giggles. But it was the image of Khaled that had stopped Lily in her tracks. An image the world would barely recognise. For there was no trace of the famously melancholy Sad Prince.

Chest liberally coated in patches of sand, ebony hair all tousled and wet, eyes brimming with mirth, he was *smiling*.

Lily just stared.

The man was already insanely handsome, but

that smile took those stunning looks to another level.

It was dazzling. *He* was dazzling.

'It's quite a shot, isn't it?' said Eleanor, entering the room. 'Bassam took it. It was the summer before his first heart attack. Our last real family holiday. A friend owns an island in the Indian Ocean. We were there for a week and Khaled and the girls just stayed out on the beach all day. I've never seen him so relaxed—before or since.'

Lily flushed, embarrassed to be caught gawping. 'It's a lovely photo.'

The Queen's eyes glittered as she led her guest to the sofas, calling over the servant holding a tray of coffee and pastries.

'If he'd unleash that smile for the cameras once in a while all that Sad Prince nonsense would go away,' Eleanor said. 'But even as a child he was a sombre little thing, following his big brother around. From the moment Khaled could walk, all he wanted was to be with Faisal. That boy was so full of life. We all adored my stepson. But he and Khaled were particularly close. After the accident he became so stern. You were young yourself, but perhaps you remember his visit a little?'

She did. She remembered the boy standing so still and grave in a room filled with sunbeams.

'You helped him a great deal, you know,' his mother said. 'We thought you would. We imagined being with another child would be easier than being with adults, and we wanted to get him away from all the press attention.'

She poured coffee, handing Lily a cup.

'It was Nate's suggestion, wasn't it?'

'Yes, clever boy. His friendship with Khaled wasn't well known at the time, so the Marchant estate was the last place anyone would have looked. He said that, left to their own devices, his "Baby Sis" and Khaled would get along famously. How right he was.'

The glitter in the Queen's eye intensified. 'And it seems those childhood bonds of yours have become even stronger in adulthood.'

'It's early days, really,' Lily said into her coffee. 'We seem to be having a lot of arguments. Quite public ones.'

Eleanor chuckled. 'You mean the grumpy workaholic remark? That was priceless! I've never seen my son at such a loss for words before.'

'I maybe went a bit too far...'

'My dear, it was no less than he deserved. I've no doubt he engineered your visit, and all the nonsense around that shopping trip, to force your hand in some way. When he wants something he goes after it with a vengeance. But you must stand firm. We're thrilled he's brought you here, but don't be coerced into something you don't want.'

So Eleanor thought Khaled was resorting to underhand tactics to secure her hand? He was forcing her hand, all right, but not the way his mother thought.

'I do hope you give him a chance, though. My son is a good man and he deserves to be happy. I think you're just what he needs.'

Lily took a gulp of coffee.

'The twins have been good for him, of course,' Eleanor said. 'He was certainly less desolate once they arrived. When Khaled was born there were complications, and we were told I'd have no more babies. At the time it was devastating, but Bassam and I were grateful for the two boys. After losing Faisal, and seeing Khaled so altered by it, we decided to take some advice. Treatment had moved on, you see. And we were fortunate to be blessed with our girls.'

'The twins have helped him?' Lily asked, grateful for the change of subject.

'Yes, although nothing has stopped him from punishing himself. He works all the time. I think he was actually glad to take on his father's responsibilities. He wants to make amends.'

'Amends?' Lily asked, surprised. 'For what?'

Eleanor's eyes misted over as she looked up at the image of her first-born child. 'For being the wrong prince to survive.'

Lily stared again at the smiling man who strove every day for the good of others and yet believed he personally had no right to exist.

'The boys and their father had gone into the

desert,' Eleanor said. 'They loved racing dune buggies. But that morning Faisal lost control of his. The poor boy. He was always a little wild…'

She trailed off, but then roused herself. 'But I didn't invite you here to get all maudlin. It's Bassam's anniversary party in a month, and I wondered if you'd consider staying with us until then. Khaled will be away in America briefly, and I know you might have plans to accompany him, but there would still be time for you to get to know the country. To see if you might like to stay permanently.'

Staying permanently wasn't an option. Lily knew that. But to stay for another month…? If she did, maybe she'd be able to help Nate? But would she emerge on the other side with her heart intact?

She was falling more and more for this place. For the kindness of Eleanor and the welcome of the family. For the heat and endless sunshine.

And…for Khaled.

The tyrant who'd melted her heart.

Who would never really have time for her.

'Please say yes. We'd be delighted to have you,' Eleanor said.

If she agreed, Khaled would be furious. After his performance this morning she'd take some pleasure in that. So before she could talk herself out of it she heard herself say, 'I'd love to.'

Eleanor clapped her hands together. 'Wonderful. Perhaps Nate will arrive in time to join us?

You know, Bassam and I were delighted when he took the job as director of the charity. He's already exceeded the initial targets. The biggest coup, of course, was recently getting all those millions from George. I never knew my cousin had any interest in conservation...'

Lily tried to hide her shock. George Hyde-Wallace had made a donation to the fund just before a chunk of it went missing? Something didn't sound right with that...

But doing anything with the information would have to wait. The girls had arrived for their promised morning by the pool.

# CHAPTER NINE

SOME HOURS LATER, Khaled was reflecting on his morning. It wasn't the worst he'd ever had—but, hell, it was up there.

First that spat outside the breakfast room, which had left him ready to snap the head off anyone who crossed him—not the best of moods for his series of morning meetings.

He'd started with a delegation from the United Nations, finalising details for his speech to the General Assembly in New York later that month. Nothing in his career to date had been more important, nor had consumed his professional life so completely, yet no less than three times Sabir had had to prompt him when his attention had wandered.

He'd actually lost his train of thought completely when he'd imagined he'd heard Lily's quick, light step approaching, and the maid bringing refreshments for his UN visitors had quailed under the Prince's fierce glare and hastily retreated after serving the guests. He'd concocted a plausible apology and had it conveyed to the woman. It wasn't her fault she'd been mistaken for Lily. But when had he learned the sound of her footsteps—and, more importantly, why was he allowing it to matter?

The second meeting had been with the Qaydari ambassador, who'd changed his tune since the last time they'd met, and had arrived with a new set of proposals, finally granting the concessions Khaled had requested. A result—or so he'd thought.

Until the man had revealed the outrageous caveat.

*If* Nabhan would meet all costs for building the new dam and its associated infrastructure.

He'd barely stopped himself from telling the ambassador where he could stick his concessions. Parading Lily as his new lover hadn't softened the King's stance at all. If anything, he'd become more demanding. And Khaled had wondered, not for the first time, if he really wanted to align himself and his country with such a man.

His anger had still been simmering when the third set of guests had walked into his *majlis*. This time from the Marsh Bedouin, to discuss the conservation work for the marshlands they depended on, and the funds raised at the recent charity launch. Five men in blue *dishdasha* and red *shemaghs*. Six, if you counted the additional surprise delegate.

A 'delegate' bearing revelatory, almost incendiary information.

He was still processing the impact of what he'd been told, and just when he thought his day couldn't get any worse…

'I have to talk to you.'

Lily bounded into his office unannounced, all

glossy hair and shapely legs. Still in those damn shorts.

Khaled scowled as he watched her drop, uninvited, into the seat opposite him. 'Were you never taught to knock before entering a room?'

'Your trained killer on the door was awfully sweet and let me through without batting an eyelid, so I assumed I was welcome.'

The man might not be on the door much longer…

'I remembered seeing him at your house in England, so we had a little catch-up. Do you know he's going to be a father for the first time in the New Year? Looks like at least one of your guards will be powdering something after all. A baby's bottom.' She giggled at her joke. 'They're having a girl. They're naming her Elnoor, after the Queen. Isn't that lovely? I said that if *we* had a girl we'd—'

He raised a staying hand. 'What exactly do you think you're doing?'

After the morning he'd had, if she said *improvising* he was going to smash something.

'Acting all happy and loved-up.' She looked puzzled. 'You said I was to be convincing. Asking about a member of staff's baby seems quite natural. We'd be planning babies, too, wouldn't we? If we were really getting engaged? But if you want me to be cool and distant let me know—though please stop changing your mind. I can't keep up with your contradictory instructions.'

A sound like someone choking back a laugh

had her spinning towards the corner of the room and the robed figure standing there. She looked horrified that she'd chattered on while Khaled still had a guest.

Then the guest winked at her.

'Nate!'

Lily jumped to her feet and ran to her stepbrother, flinging herself into his waiting arms, bestowing her most dazzling smile on him.

Khaled ground his teeth. If she'd used that on the guard, no wonder he'd been so amenable.

'Hey, Baby Sis.'

'Where have you've been? What happened to you? Are you okay?'

She fired questions at him, patting his chest all the while, as if checking he was in one piece.

'I'm fine. I've been hiding with the Marsh Bedouin. They're good friends.'

Khaled watched the exchange and experienced a new and most unwelcome emotion. He was being ridiculous. Nate was her brother.

*Stepbrother*, an invidious little voice reminded him, and no blood relation.

He had to curb the impulse to march over there and haul her away from his friend.

Then his attention caught on what she was saying.

'So we can end this pretend relationship?'

'No!'

Stepbrother and sister turned as one to stare at

him. Nate's eyes were glinting in unholy amusement at his emphatic response.

'I mean,' Khaled said, being careful to sound more measured this time, 'it's safer for Nate if we continue until we can prove who's behind the theft.'

'Plus, I've already given my consent,' Nate said.

Lily looked at him, aghast. 'You've done *what*? I don't need your consent.'

'That's not what you said to the press.' Nate grinned at her.

'That was a ruse. You know this whole thing isn't real. And in the eligibility stakes isn't he a bit out of my league.'

'You're the granddaughter of a duke.'

'Estranged granddaughter,' she reminded him.

Nate shrugged. 'Makes no difference. You have a legitimate aristocratic heritage going back generations. Much further back than his. There could be no objection to your marriage.'

'Except that he's a tyrant,' Lily muttered.

The tyrant lounged in his chair. Broad-shouldered, divinely handsome.

Even if their relationship were real she wouldn't marry him. His wife would be side-lined over and over in the name of royal duty. But in a dark, locked-away corner somewhere, a part of her still reached for him. For his heat and his strength and all the things he could make her feel.

His hand rested on the desk, fingers slowly drumming. She shivered. Those fingers were magic.

Their eyes clashed. His gleamed. He knew exactly what she'd been thinking.

'Is there a purpose to your visit?' he said.

Purpose…

What was it again? Oh, yes.

Big donation.

Queen's cousin.

Theft.

She sat up straighter. 'I think George Hyde-Wallace is behind the theft.'

'Yeah, we know,' said Nate bitterly. 'He's been boasting to one of his cronies that I'll soon be gone from Khaled's inner circle and that Khaled's going to have to start toeing the line or risk being ousted. And by "toeing the line" he means dropping all attempts at reforming the role of the Council of Families, which means George will maintain his hold on power. The traitorous bastard.'

'How do you know all this?' Lily asked.

'George believes he has the entire Council in his pocket. He's wrong,' Khaled said darkly.

'But it's all hearsay. We can't prove a thing,' Nate added. 'He's covered his tracks too well.'

'Then call his bluff to draw him out. Make a big deal of the Hyde-Wallace donation and start on the projects the money was raised for. If the funds are being used as intended, how can he cry foul without revealing that he knew something already.'

'You're missing the essential point,' Khaled said. 'The money is gone.'

'Only ten million—I'm sure you're good for it.'

'But if the theft becomes public it will look like I covered it up and Hyde-Wallace will discredit me anyway.'

'Then your plan needs the sanction of someone in the highest of places,' Lily said.

Khaled looked blank.

She rolled her eyes. 'Duh. Your father. Who would dare question the word of the King?'

'You know, that idea's got legs,' Nate said. 'Why didn't we come up with that yesterday?'

Lily's flush of pride was forgotten. 'What do you mean, yesterday?'

Nate frowned at Khaled. 'You didn't tell her we'd spoken?'

It was like a slap to her face. 'You were talking to my stepbrother yesterday and you didn't let me know last night, or at any point since? When you know how worried I've been?'

'I wasn't entirely convinced. I needed to check Nate's story,' Khaled said, not the least repentant.

She rounded on her stepbrother. 'Why are you even friends with this man? He hasn't an ounce of trust in his body.'

'I'm a prince. I don't have that luxury,' Khaled said.

'To be fair, Baby Sis,' Nate added, 'the evidence against me was pretty damning.'

'Don't you dare defend him. Do you know, while he's parading me around as his pretend fiancée, he's already promised himself to a foreign princess?'

She was ashamed now of her antics in front of the journalists. She'd meant to embarrass Khaled, not some poor woman who was apparently just as much a pawn in all this as she.

'There was no need for you to know that. It would have only complicated matters,' Khaled said coolly.

'Too right. I would have said no.' She glared at him. 'Dragging me halfway round the world… Using me as bait… You really are the lowest kind of man.'

His jaw tightened. 'I won't tolerate your insolence in here.'

'You don't have to. I'm leaving. Take care, Nate, and stay in touch.' She pecked him on the cheek.

'Where are you going?' Khaled demanded.

'I thought I might look at engagement rings.' She held out her left hand, waggling her naked ring finger. 'I'm thinking something brash and showy that's trying to look like a diamond but is actually fake. In other words, a big fat liar. Just like you.' Lily glared at him. 'Two fiancées at the same time? What a gallant way to treat women. Your mother and sisters must be so proud.'

Then she turned on her heel and headed for the door, leaving the handsome tyrant to stew.

# CHAPTER TEN

THE BEACH THAT ran beside the palace looked much like any other stretch of Nabhani shoreline. Except for the soldiers patrolling the perimeter and the steel-grey gunboat skimming the waves in the near distance.

This stretch of perfect ivory sand was reserved for the sole use of the royal family and its guests.

After Lily had stomped into the family room the Queen had diplomatically suggested her current guest might appreciate some time to herself there, beyond the dunes, where she wouldn't be disturbed. In the late afternoon they benefitted from a cooling breeze, she'd told her, and in her opinion were rather restful.

Lily, too angry to be good company, had thought it an excellent suggestion. So now, in a bikini and a loose shirt, shaded by the brim of a sun hat, she sat beneath an umbrella in the lee of one of the larger dunes.

She still seethed about Khaled's lies, and how he'd hidden from her the fact that Nate was safe. And jealousy was gnawing away at her, too, and she hated herself for it. Somewhere out there a young woman waited, destined to be Khaled's bride, to share his bed, to know his touch.

Aisha might be in love with him. If her affections weren't returned, would she be doomed to a half-life, dwindling away, yearning for the attentions of a man who would never put her first? Because he was a world leader, with hard choices to make and little room for softness of the heart?

Except Lily remembered a day when he'd been more than kind to her...

After her mother's wake.

Khaled had been leaving, and as they'd crossed the hall on the way to his car he'd seen a pile of that day's newspapers on a table in plain view. Her mother's image had been splashed across every front page. In a rage he'd snatched them up and dumped every one of them in a wastebasket. Then he'd dropped to his haunches and begged her, on no account, to look at any of them. She'd promised him she wouldn't and put her arms about his neck.

'Good girl,' he'd said, and squeezed her tight.

But later, when the house had been quiet, she'd crept downstairs and taken those newspapers into the library. She'd read every one and cried in hurt and humiliation. They'd published the worst photographs, the most shaming stories. Stories she'd never heard before.

How her mother had been fired from her last film for turning up hours late and forgetting her lines. How she'd been thrown off a flight, blind drunk, foul-mouthed and fighting with the security staff who had been attempting to keep her and the other passengers safe.

And, worst of all, how she'd neglected her only child.

But nobody knew that once, before her husband had chosen his career over them, and broken her heart, she'd sat with her daughter in the mornings, softly singing to her and brushing and untangling her hair with deft, gentle fingers.

Lily had torn the papers to shreds and then run upstairs to her mother's room. The pills, the tumblers and the empty vodka bottles had all been cleared away. But on the dressing table had sat the ebony and silver hairbrush.

Lily had snatched it up, climbed into her mother's bed, and cried herself to sleep.

The next day Edward had left for London, and she'd gone to school and pretended that none of it mattered. Because hadn't she really lost her mother years ago?

She'd gone to her classes. Sat with friends at lunch. Caught the school bus home to an empty house and eaten the meal the housekeeper had left for her. She'd tidied the kitchen, done her homework, then got herself ready for bed. Like she did any other day.

Pretending none of it mattered.

Except that tucked away in the bottom of her school bag, carefully wrapped in an old handkerchief, was the ebony hairbrush with silver inlays and long strands of deep red hair caught in its bristles.

Lily closed her eyes on those bitter memories. She should have listened to Khaled and never read those stories. He'd tried to protect her. He'd been kind.

A thundering sound reached her. Not from the sea. From behind her—from the dunes. She sat up. It was coming her way…and fast.

She scrambled to her feet and reached the path between the banks of sand just as a horse and rider galloped out of it.

The startled horse reared up, its thrashing hooves missing her head by inches. Lily lurched backwards, tripped on a piece of driftwood, and landed flat on her backside. In her panic, she scuttled backwards, staring in horror as the rider sawed at the reins, working to get the animal under control.

At last the horse was calmed. Its rider flung himself from the saddle. 'Lily, my God, are you hurt?'

Khaled.

Looking magnificent in white shirt, skin-tight riding breeches and long leather boots, his head swathed in a checked *shemagh*.

Grateful for the cover of her hat's brim, because one glimpse of him had sent heat to her cheeks, Lily struggled to her feet. 'I'm okay,' she spluttered.

Did he always have to look so gorgeous?

'What the hell do you think you were doing, running in front of a horse like that?'

Typical—the concern had lasted about a nano-second and now he was angry at her.

'Enjoying some peace and quiet—until you came pounding up on that horrible beast. If I'd known anyone was riding out here I would never have come— Ow!'

She couldn't stop the yelp of pain as she placed her full weight on her left ankle.

'You are injured?' One hand arrived beneath her elbow, the other curled about her waist.

'It's nothing,' she protested, acutely aware of his touch through her flimsy shirt.

'Let me look at it.' He dropped to one knee beside her. 'Put your hand on my shoulder.'

He waited until she'd obeyed and leant her weight against him, before lifting her damaged foot.

There was the heady scent of fresh male sweat, and beneath her fingers Lily felt the shift of solid muscle as he worked. Yet he was infinitely gentle as he carefully manipulated the joint.

'I don't think it's serious, but the sooner we get some ice on that the better.' He rose up. 'I'll take you back with me.'

The allure of the man beside her was forgotten as Lily glanced at the black monster tossing its head. Her heart pounded as Khaled swept past her, scooped her few possessions into a neat pile on the lounger, then strode back to grasp the horse's reins.

'Really, I'll be fine. I'll take it slowly,' she said, trying her weight again and gasping at a fresh stab of pain.

'Don't be ridiculous. You can't even walk.'

In one swift move he was back in the saddle, with a ripple of muscle and power that had her heart racing faster still. He edged the horse closer.

'What about my things?' she asked, stalling. Anything to avoid getting on that animal.

'Someone will be sent for them.' He stretched out his hand.

'Won't the people on the boat out there have seen what's happened and send help?'

Khaled peered at the grey shape out on the waves. 'Not if they value their positions. The security teams don't set foot on this beach unless they perceive a genuine threat. They'll only approach at a sign from me.'

'Then couldn't you wave to them?'

He turned cool grey eyes on her. 'You want me to wave at a gunboat and scramble security for a twisted ankle? Besides, in the time it takes for a Jeep to get here we could be back in the palace. That ankle needs treatment. The quickest route is back through the dunes.'

The horse, getting impatient, pawed at the sand with a great hoof.

Seeing her shrink back, Khaled said, 'You've

nothing to be afraid of. I'm the master here. He does as he's bid.'

And didn't that sound as much about her doing as she was told as the beast he sat upon?

But the animal was obeying him, and beyond her mistrust of it came a far more tangible sensation. Her ankle had started throbbing. Getting ice on it seemed appealing right now.

Steeling herself, Lily squeezed her eyes shut, stretched out a hand, and felt the ground fall away as she soared upwards.

It was the fear, Khaled decided. It had robbed him of his good sense. First the horror of watching Lily disappear beneath Mu'tazz's hooves, and then seeing her in pain.

His only thought had been to get her to a doctor. He just hadn't considered the implications of having her perched, practically naked, in his lap, and how good it would feel to hold her close. Or that she in turn would cling to him so fiercely out of a fear of her own, foisting upon him another inconvenient emotion: the urge to protect her.

Perhaps he should have hailed the gunboat. They'd have sent someone soon enough and he'd have avoided all this.

Because now Khaled realised his second mistake. Something he'd quite forgotten in his haste to get Lily back to the palace. Something that explained her reluctance to approach Mu'tazz and why her hands were now desperately knotted in his shirtfront, her face hidden in his neck.

Too late, he remembered the fearless little girl who'd been afraid of only one thing—who'd always stayed safely behind fences whenever he'd taken her brother's mare out in the paddock. The girl whose father had died in a riding accident.

He felt her tremble and pulled her closer, cursing his inattention.

Horses. They terrified her.

Mu'tazz shifted his weight and a new shudder went through her.

'Please can we hurry?'

Her muffled plea came from deep in the folds of his *shemagh*.

He wanted to be angry with her. He'd abandoned work for the day because he'd been achieving precisely nothing. When she'd stormed out on him earlier he'd wanted to go after her, kiss her, touch her until she came apart for him again. Instead he'd come out here to ride, to the point of exhaustion if necessary—whatever it took to banish Lily Marchant from his mind.

But here she was, hurt, frightened, and he was to blame.

He gathered up the reins, folding her tighter against him. 'You're safe. I promise.'

The stallion began walking on command. Lily whimpered and shifted even closer. Her rump pressed into his groin, evoking memories of what had happened the last time she sat in his lap.

Khaled gritted his teeth. He needed something to distract them both.

'Did you know our fathers met?' he blurted.

He felt her start of surprise, but she didn't look up.

'Bassam knew my dad?' she asked.

'Met him,' he corrected. 'My father said it was only briefly. At a garden party in England. But you were with him at the time.'

The death grip on his shirtfront eased a fraction. 'I was?' She peeked up at him from beneath the brim of her hat. 'He's sure it was me?'

'He said that all the time they were speaking your father had a little girl with unforgettable red hair sitting on his shoulders.'

'"Unforgettable red hair"?' she grumbled. 'That sounds like me, all right.'

A wistful look clouded her eyes. It reached into his chest and closed tight about his heart.

'Perhaps that's where my memory of him comes from,' she said. 'I remember sitting on a man's shoulders. We were having fun. Apart from with Nate, it's one of the few times I ever felt like someone really wanted me around. But that can't really be true, can it? Because in the end he abandoned my mother and me to chase his career.'

Mu'tazz navigated a dip in the path and his riders swayed in the saddle. But that wasn't the reason for the tightening of the protective arm about Lily's waist, nor for the tender glance directed to the top of her head.

'Even though that's true, I still miss him, you know?'

'Yes, I do,' Khaled answered, reminded of his own loss, of the agony of having a beloved brother wrenched from him.

It was curious how being close to this girl eased that pain. Guilt nagged at him. He should have eased her anxieties over her stepbrother yesterday.

'It was wrong of me. Not telling you I'd spoken with Nate. I apologise.'

She looked up sharply. He allowed one corner of his mouth to lift.

Her eyes narrowed on him, but then she slumped back against his chest. 'I know what you're trying to do. You're trying to charm me so I forget to be cross with you.'

'What a dastardly and devious thing to do,' he said, and after a pause asked, 'Is it working?'

He heard a huff of irritation, but the trembling of her shoulders told him she was laughing.

'You know you're incorrigible?'

'That's actually a desirable skill in my line of work.'

She laughed again, then cautiously reached out to touch the horse's thick neck muscle. 'What's he called?'

'Mu'tazz.' On hearing his name, the stallion's ears twitched. 'And he's fond of neck-rubs.'

She scratched her fingers back and forth. 'Maybe he's not as frightening as I first thought.'

'Back there he was probably more terrified of you than you were of him.'

'I doubt that,' she said, but he noticed she was stroking the glossy black mane, slowly curling one strand over and over in her slender fingers. He looked elsewhere as need shimmered over his skin.

'Will you tell me something?' she asked.

Right now he'd gladly talk about anything. 'What do you want to know?'

'About Aisha. I mean, why her?'

'Because of who her father is. An alliance with Qaydar will have benefits for the people here.' Not that he was quite so certain of that any more.

'So what were you hoping to gain by pretending I'm your girlfriend?'

No harm in sharing that with her now, and he realised that he trusted her. 'Her father has been dragging his heels on certain details. I thought seeing you on my arm might prompt him back to the negotiating table.'

'And never mind if Aisha gets hurt?'

'It's not that kind of arrangement. Emotion doesn't come into it.'

'Spoken like the one with all the power. If she's going to be your wife, don't you think she'll want to be chosen first—you know…for her? Not because of the mountain range she happens to live by.'

'Aisha has been raised as a royal. She understands how these things work.'

She muttered something indistinct and fell silent.

Up ahead the entrance to the stable block came into view, and he felt an odd ripple of energy go through her. But those fingers still idly twirled in Mu'tazz's mane. He tried not to stare. He was *not* envious of his damn horse.

'I suppose now you've apologised to me,' she said, 'it's only fair that I should say I'm sorry, too. About how I've behaved in all this. I know you're in a difficult position, and that you really are trying to protect Nate.'

She looked at him, her hazel eyes genuinely contrite, and to his surprise she reached up and kissed his cheek. It was nothing more than a simple peck, but it set his pulse racing.

When her lashes lowered, and her gaze dropped to his lips, he couldn't prevent the hitch in his breathing. She touched her mouth to his. A brief buss of soft lips.

Like some breathless untried teenager he swallowed. She traced the movement of his throat with her fingertips and he shuddered as desire surged through him.

He pulled her close.

Too rough. She hissed in pain. The movement had wrenched her injured ankle.

'I'm sorry, I—'

'Shh, it's all right.'

She laid her palm tenderly against his jaw, as if it was he who needed soothing. Then her hand went higher, pushing the *shemagh* backwards so her fingers could tangle in his hair.

He groaned and, carefully this time, drew her nearer. The warm mounds of her breasts, the sharp peaks of her nipples pressed against his chest. The smell of her and the sea breeze mingled together, and he couldn't tell where one ended and the other began.

He gave himself up to the kiss…to her.

Slender fingers tightened around his skull, holding his face to hers, but nothing would have induced him to pull away. He never wanted to come up for air again. He didn't care about breathing. He needed this more.

A sound intruded nearby. Whatever it was, he'd ignore it. This woman was all that mattered.

His hands spread possessively across her back.

Someone cleared his throat, and then again, louder.

On a growl of frustration, Khaled lifted his head. To discover they were in the centre of the stable courtyard, surrounded by goggling stable hands, and with them was Rais, inscrutable as ever.

In the absence of any other command, Mu'tazz, had simply plodded home.

'The team on the boat called it in, sir. The doctor is waiting,' his security chief said, walking up to take Lily. 'If you will permit me, Miss Marchant?'

She unwound her arms from Khaled's neck.

'Oops. Looks like we wandered into an audience and you had no idea. Not nice, is it?' she whispered, and then shifted to allow Rais to lift her down and carry her away.

His blood roaring, his heart racing, Khaled watched her go. Leaving him how? Aroused. Conflicted. Out-played.

She'd used that sweet, giving mouth and delectable body to distract him, to lure him back here and serve him up his own medicine. The little madam. She'd probably claim she'd been 'improvising'.

Suddenly, and much to the astonishment of the grooms, he threw back his head and laughed. She constantly challenged his authority, tested his patience—but, by God, the woman made him feel awake.

Climbing that ivy. Breaking into his rooms. Standing up to him and fighting him every step of the way. She had some nerve. And some loyalty. Believing absolutely in her stepbrother and doing everything in her power to help him.

A woman like that would make a damn fine consort for any man.

Khaled slid from the saddle, gave Mu'tazz an affectionate, if absent-minded pat, and handed the reins to a stable lad. As he walked he considered the Qaydaris and their slippery negotiating. Would an alliance with them be more trouble than it was worth? Would he come to regret it? And did that change his options?

What if his marriage created no problems of that kind? What if, instead of Aisha, he took an English girl, with nothing to offer but an aristocratic lineage and the delight of her body?

Feeling energised, taking the stairs to his rooms three at a time, he began to wonder.

What if...?

Was it crazy?

What if he genuinely chose Lily Marchant to be his wife?

# CHAPTER ELEVEN

TWENTY MINUTES LATER, towelling himself dry after a shower, Khaled decided he'd found the perfect solution to the question of his marriage.

Marry Lily and there'd be no awkward father-in-law to placate. No risk of poor chemistry between husband and wife. He was physically drawn to her, and that kiss they'd shared hadn't been all for show on her part. She'd get as much satisfaction from the marriage bed as he would.

She seemed unfazed by palace life. She'd even handled their encounter with the press. With guidance from his mother, he had no doubt she'd be able to manage the demands of being his princess.

Better still, his strange yearning, this inconvenient concern for her, would disappear. They were just the symptoms of sexual frustration. His focus and concentration would return and he would be able to get on with being the Crown Prince.

God knew, that was the least he owed to his father.

As ever, on the next breath, Faisal came to mind. What would he have advised?

With a clench of pain, he recognised the question was irrelevant. The advice would have been going the other way. His brother should have been choosing the next Crown Princess of Nabhan.

Brooding on that, when the phone rang he answered automatically—and cursed himself when he recognised the caller.

'My apologies for disturbing you,' said George Hyde-Wallace, his tone, as always, hovering just on the wrong side of deferential. 'I understand Miss Marchant has been injured and I want to offer the assistance of my personal physician.'

Khaled bit his tongue. He knew for certain now that Hyde-Wallace was definitely plotting against him. And the endless impertinence of the man. As if the royal family didn't have access to the finest doctors already.

'It's merely a twisted ankle,' he said, waiting for the real purpose of this call.

'I'm relieved to hear it. Such a charming young woman. You seem to be growing rather fond of her yourself. Some are even suggesting you might propose to the girl—though of course sadly that's impossible. The Constitution forbids it.'

'The *Constitution*?'

'Lily Marchant is illegitimate.'

As a shock tactic, the statement was masterful. It rendered Khaled temporarily speechless.

Illegitimate? It couldn't be true. Her parents had been married. Famously so. It was what had cut them off from her father's family. But icy shards pricked along his spine. George was too careful to make a claim like that without evidence.

'And you know this how?' he said eventually, as casually as he could.

'I've always had my concerns about Nathaniel Marchant, so I had him and his stepsister investigated some time ago. For your protection, of course.'

*Yeah, right.*

'It turns out her parents' romantic beach wedding was merely a handfasting performed by an unlicensed celebrant. Certainly not legal in Nabhan. However, in light of your interest in the girl, I've taken the precaution of concealing what I've discovered from anyone else who bothers to look. For now.'

Khaled didn't miss that tagged-on veiled threat.

For only the second time in his life he experienced a feeling of utter impotency. There was nothing to be done if this were true, because George was right. The Constitution forbade such a marriage. The requirement has been built in to it to ensure peace amongst Nabhan's senior families. Both monarch and consort must be legitimate.

But George hadn't finished. 'It would be terrible if this information reached the press... I imagine it would destroy her. All those stories about her disgrace of a mother would resurface... There would be no chance of reconciliation with her grandfather... Apart from that stepbrother of hers, she would be completely alone.'

His thoughts landed with a ferocious determination. *She would not be alone. She would have me.*

But how? How could Khaled stand between her and harm when the best way to protect her from George's threats was to push her away.

'May I suggest a solution?' George drawled into the silence. 'Announce your engagement to the Qaydari Princess and the media will quickly shift their interest. Who would bother to search any further into Miss Marchant's background then? Her reputation would be safe.'

And George would have a powerful ally against Khaled's reforms in the shape of the conservative King of Qaydar.

'I'll leave you to ponder on that. Perhaps we could meet later, to discuss what you've decided? Shall we say before dinner this evening?'

Without waiting for a response, George ended the call.

First the theft. Now this. Hyde-Wallace was using whatever means he could to try and control Khaled.

As for Lily...

So be it. It was a passing infatuation anyway.

And that stab of anguish at the thought of letting her go? That would pass, too.

He'd make it appear that their affair had ended. Suggest they'd had a falling-out. A terminal one. But while the theft remained unresolved it would be safer if she stayed in Nabhan. He'd leave her in the palace with his family, say that she was staying on as a guest of his mother and sisters while he removed himself from the country.

He wasn't due in New York for another three weeks. But there was little in his diary before then that he couldn't just as easily do using New York or London as his base. It was almost a month before he'd need to return for his father's anniversary party. A month ought to do it.

He swept up the phone again, to instruct Sabir to make the arrangements.

He was leaving for Europe tonight.

'No bones broken, young lady. It's just a sprain and should mend in a few days.' The doctor gathered his bag, getting ready to leave Lily's suite. 'Alternate ice and heat to help with the swelling, and walk as much as you can, hmm? Use that if necessary.' He pointed to the crutch just delivered from the palace sick bay.

Lily wondered if he could have so easily prescribed something for her other symptoms. The racing heart, the breathlessness, the feeling that she was on the edge of a precipice and could just as easily fly as fall...

Why, *why* had she been so stupid as to kiss Khaled again? Because now she could think of nothing else. Her plan for revenge had seriously backfired.

She left the twins, who were busy organising

ice packs and footstools for her neatly bandaged ankle, and hobbled to the bathroom, to change and wash away the grime from the beach.

When she re-emerged, she found Eleanor had arrived and Amal was excitedly recounting the details of her accident.

'Khaled brought her back on his horse.'

Eleanor's eyes glowed. 'On Mu'tazz? Oh, that is romantic.'

Eager to change the subject, Lily said, 'Hanan mentioned you're having a beach barbecue tonight. That sounds lovely. I hope I can get there?'

'Don't worry—Khaled can carry you!' Hanan sniggered.

'If he joins us at all. Girls, why don't you go and invite him? You might be able to persuade him.' Eleanor's indulgent smile for her daughters became wistful. 'We know he'll work all evening otherwise.'

'I'll go,' Lily said, reaching for the crutch.

'Are you sure, dear? He'll be in his office. It's quite a walk.'

'The doctor said I should try to use the ankle.'

She took a few tentative steps. With the crutch it wasn't so hard. Either way, she needed to move.

She felt so restless. A thrilling image of Khaled carrying her to the beach had come too easily to mind. She knew precisely how it felt to be in arms, how easily he could lift her, the potent strength of him.

She stabbed the crutch down. Ridiculous to be salivating over how strong he was when she should be remembering the pertinent facts in all this. He'd used her to force another monarch back to the negotiating table so he could wring better terms from the man.

Even so, she was ashamed of how she'd behaved this afternoon. Playing the same trick on him he'd used on her didn't make things right. She needed to apologise.

But she'd badly overestimated how far she could walk. By the time she reached the office suites her ankle was in agony. It must have shown on her face. The guard on the door took pity on her, leading her straight into Khaled's office.

It was empty, though she was assured the Prince had only stepped out for a moment. On his desk sat an open laptop and a scatter of papers.

She sank into Khaled's chair, reaching down to rub her aching ankle, and found she was at eye level with the framed photo she'd noticed yesterday.

It was not of his parents or sisters, or Mu'tazz, but of two young men. The older of the two, grinning broadly, had his arm slung across the other's shoulder. Both had the same luxuriant ebony hair and strong, determined chin. The younger had pale grey eyes.

Brothers.

Faisal and Khaled.

The grey-eyed boy was so like the teenager she'd first met she knew the photo must have been taken close to that time. He was still unsmiling, but there was no sadness there. She thought of the other image she'd seen today, and of the stunning smile this boy, as a man, would hardly use.

The sun had set and the room, lit only by the desk lamp, was wreathed in shadows. But from the farthest of the bookshelves behind her came a dull glimmer. It was the gold-lettered spines of the little collection she'd spied yesterday. Unable to resist, she hitched herself out of the chair, limped over and bent closer to study their titles.

*The Adventures of Huckleberry Finn, Wind in the Willows, Treasure Island...* Classic children's books. A dozen or so.

Even more curious now, she slipped two from the shelf and hobbled back to her seat. She angled one under the light and opened it to the first page, to find a neat handwritten dedication.

*For Faisal on his tenth birthday.*
*With fondest love from Grandpa Wallace*

The second book held a similar message, this time for Faisal's eleventh birthday.

The breath caught in her throat.

Amidst all the scholarly texts and professional journals, in an office devoid of any other personal touches, Khaled kept his brother's photo and his childhood books.

'You seem to have great trouble respecting my privacy.'

Lily jumped, snapping the book closed.

Khaled filled the doorway.

Awareness flooded through her, along with a sensitivity in her breasts and her thighs, as if her clothes had suddenly become too tight.

But in that same instant she recognised that she'd been intruding on something deeply personal to him and, ashamed of herself, babbled an apology. 'I'm so sorry. I was just looking at the books while I waited.'

He glanced to her hands and his face contorted. In four strides he reached her and wrenched the books from her fingers. He returned them to the shelf, then took up station by the window. Arms folded, legs planted wide, he stared into the blank darkness beyond.

She struggled to her feet. 'I didn't mean to pry,' she said to his back, 'but I've always loved old books and those are so beautiful.'

He ignored her explanation. 'What exactly are you here for?'

'I came to apologise.'

Over his shoulder, he stared at her. 'For which particular transgression? There have been so many.'

'The kiss…at the stable block.'

He shrugged. 'Why? We enjoyed it and we both know it meant nothing. But if it makes you feel better I accept your apology. Now, if you will excuse me, I have work to do.'

Confused by the change in him from just an hour ago, Lily stumbled on. 'But…but your mother hoped you'd join the family for dinner on the beach.'

He gave a dismissive snort. 'Please pass my apologies to my mother, but I've no time. I'm leaving for England in an hour.'

'England?'

'Yes.' He shot her an odd glance, loaded with a meaning she couldn't decipher. 'I know you've been invited to remain here until my father's anniversary party, and after reconsidering I think that could be useful. Until we can categorically prove your stepbrother's innocence, more speculation about us won't hurt.'

Why was he so angry? Just because of the books?

'You may go,' he said, and when she still didn't move he snapped, *'Now.'*

Shocked and hurt by that curt dismissal, Lily lashed out. 'To think I actually felt sorry for you because you keep your brother's things close by. But I'll save my sympathy for Aisha. She deserves it.' She grabbed the crutch and hobbled round the desk. Her ankle throbbed, but she just wanted to get out of there. 'How do you live with yourself?' she demanded. 'Don't you feel any guilt at all?'

There was a flash of movement by the window and she felt a new tension in the room, as if the air had become electrified. He moved towards her, halting so close she had to tip her head back to meet his glittering gaze.

'You dare speak to me of guilt?' All the shadows in the room seemed to coalesce around him. 'It's burned into my soul. It curses my very existence. But I keep Faisal's things close by in case I'm ever tempted to forget.'

'Because you survived and he didn't?' Lily whispered.

His beautiful mouth twisted into a cruel sneer. 'Oh, every damn psychologist my mother dragged me to said precisely that. They thought they knew the story. You all do,' he said bitterly.

'Your brother lost control of a dune buggy and there was an accident...'

'Ah, yes, that accident. Caused by my poor *reckless* brother. Everyone was so ready to blame him.' He grasped her shoulders, dragging her closer. 'But shall I tell you what really happened that day?'

When he closed his eyes he could still see it. At the base of the dune the wheels of the upturned buggy spinning wildly and Faisal, his head at a sickening angle, lying motionless in the sand.

He never had been able to remember how he'd got down that slope. Days of dull pain in his left flank suggested that he'd pitched headlong at some point, but all he knew was that one minute he was at the top of the ridge and the next he was on his knees in the sand, staring into his brother's lifeless eyes.

How long had he knelt there, his mouth open in a yawning cavern of grief? Minutes? Hours? A lifetime of agony had been compressed into those moments.

At some point arms had enveloped him. Gently urged him to his feet. Turned him away from that broken body and held him.

His father. Comforting his only surviving son. An embrace he almost hadn't been able to bear, because in it had been the forgiveness he could never deserve.

'Faisal always won,' he told Lily. 'Whatever we did, he always won. It drove me crazy, and for once I wanted to prove I was better. If I'd known how sheer the drop was on the other side of that dune I would never have done it. But I pushed and I pushed, and I drove him too close to the edge. My father knew. I heard him say the words to Rais. It was to stay between the three of us. It was an accident. We'd say Faisal had been driving too fast. But it was a lie. A terrible lie. My brother wasn't reckless. He was fearless. Because of me, even that distinction was stolen from him. All this—' he threw a contemptuous glance around them '—is a sham. It should have been his. I stole his birthright and I didn't even have the guts to make my father tell the truth.'

He saw her gaze flicker through the room. Finally she was understanding the starkness of it. There was nothing that spoke of his status. It wasn't his to make his own.

'Every day I work to ease my father's burden. It's the only thing I can do. I know his grief for Faisal burns sharp in him and he never stops feeling his loss. But still I see him watching me, willing me to forgive myself. He doesn't know the torture that is. He's trying to pour life back into me when it's too late. I'm already dead inside.'

Lily gave a strange gasping sob.

*Yes, here it comes*, he thought in bitter triumph. *The revulsion, the loathing, the innocence dying in her gaze as she looks at me.*

Even though it struck at him like daggers, he embraced the pain of it, determined to drive home every last word, so she truly understood what kind of worthless creature stood before her.

He bared his teeth in a snarl. 'I killed him, Lily. I killed my brother. And guilt is the only thing I feel any more.'

Lily stared into his eyes and saw such torment in their depths she knew she was staring right into the dark and damaged soul of the Sad Prince.

Perhaps he'd meant to frighten or repulse her with his confession, but after glimpsing the despair behind the ice-cold facade she felt only the most profound compassion.

'Oh, Khaled,' she said softly. 'All these years… What a terrible burden you've had to bear. But you loved your brother. You didn't mean to hurt him. You don't deserve to be so unhappy.'

He gave a bark of ugly laughter. 'I deserve nothing less than the torment I've suffered every day since.'

'No, you don't.' Her hands unfurled and she pressed their warmth against his chest. His brow creased, his gaze dropping to where her fingers splayed across his shirt. 'It's time to forgive yourself. It's time you had peace,' she said.

His gaze flew back to hers and a violent shudder went through him. His fingers tightened, digging into her soft flesh. 'Lily, you've no concept of all the things I may not have.'

Then his mouth crashed down on hers.

The kiss was wild, not gentle. But she kissed him back, though her lips felt bruised and his grip on her shoulders was only just not painful.

He gave a low, agonised groan and crushed her hard against him. The crutch clattered to the floor as he lifted her from her feet. He carried her to the desk and laid her on it. Papers were scattered. His laptop landed on its side in the chair. The precious photo toppled.

Lily hardly noticed. Their kiss this afternoon had been nothing compared to this. That had been a summer breeze. This was a firestorm of need, obliterating her awareness of anything other than the heat and weight of him stretching over her.

She moaned at the dark pleasure of it and in frustration—because this wasn't enough. She wanted more.

They grappled with each other. Greedy lips and frenzied, groping hands wanting to touch everything, everywhere at once.

He hitched her skirt to her waist, his palms sliding along her bare thighs. She tugged his shirttails free, her fingers finding the warm, silken skin of his back. He sighed into her mouth and sent his hands on more discoveries of their own, reaching between them to pop the buttons of her dress.

His hand slipped beneath the fabric and closed about a lace-covered breast. Her hands flew upwards, fisting in the dark silk of his hair when he wrenched the lace aside and closed his mouth around a tightly budded nipple.

'I'm afraid His Highness is occupied at present. I'll tell him you wish to speak with him, sir.'

Sabir's raised voice came clearly, in English, from the *majlis*.

Khaled lurched away. He'd straightened his shirt and smoothed his disordered hair before she'd even gathered her wits enough to push herself upright. She shuffled her bottom off the edge of the desk and balanced awkwardly on her good leg. With trembling, clumsy fingers she tidied herself, righting her bra, refastening buttons, pushing her dress down.

Khaled set the desk to rights and then, taking her elbow, helped her towards the sofa. He retrieved the crutch, placing it within her reach, and made sure she was seated, with her face, her swollen lips and her flushed cheeks directed away from the door, before he summoned Sabir.

The secretary entered at once. Had he witnessed how they had been practically ravishing each other and retreated to the *majlis* to stand guard? Lily's face flamed.

'Hyde-Wallace?' said Khaled.

'Yes, sir.'

'Gone?'

'Yes, sir.'

A muscle pulsed in Khaled's jaw.

'I'll go now and find him.'

She stared up at him in disbelief. He couldn't confess what he had, kiss her like that, and then simply walk away.

But he avoided her eye and spoke to Sabir. 'Miss Marchant has wrenched her ankle again. I don't want her walking back to her suite unaided. Organise someone to help.'

'There's a wheelchair in the sick bay. I'll have it brought round,' Sabir said.

Once he'd disappeared to make the arrangements Khaled turned to her. He looked ravaged.

'Lily, what I just did was unforgivable.'

His regret rolled over her like a winter fog. She hugged herself, rubbing her shoulders to ward off the chill.

'I have hurt you?' He sounded appalled.

'No.' She swiftly dropped her hands into her lap. 'I'm fine.'

It was a lie. She wasn't fine. Her body raged at the loss of him. Her heart broke for the pain in him. And that voice of experience she'd just ignored completely berated her.

*Give of yourself and see what happens. Rejection. Have you learned nothing?*

'Lily…' He thrust a hand through his hair and stared at her helplessly. 'I'm sorry,' he said at last. Then spun away, striding unevenly from the room.

Sabir reappeared, quietly announcing that a servant was coming to help her back to her suite. Ever the consummate aide, he didn't press her for an answer, leaving her to her thoughts. Perhaps he understood as well as she just what had happened…

Khaled had confessed his darkest secret to her, but when she'd offered emotional comfort he'd rejected that, taking something entirely more basic. Then he'd fled in shame.

Did a girl need any more humiliating evidence of where she stood in his affections?

Lily closed her eyes and fought back the welling of scalding, bitter tears.

# CHAPTER TWELVE

KHALED'S CAR ARRIVED at ten minutes after midnight, gliding through the palace gates with little ceremony. Today was the day of his father's anniversary party. In a few hours the preparations would make this entrance a bustling thoroughfare. For now, a routine snap to attention by the guards and a single aide stepping forward as the car drew to a halt was the extent of his welcome home.

Exactly as he'd ordered.

He wasn't ready to face his family.

Or the family friends starting to fill the guest suites.

Or the single occupant of the most comfortable guest suite of all.

It was almost a month since he'd absented himself from his home to keep Lily safe. Hoping, too, that physical distance would lessen the craving he felt for her.

It had not.

Desire still burned like a fever in his blood. As fiery now as when he'd left her that evening, with the taste of her on his lips and the imprint of her hot little hands on his skin.

Every day, even though he'd plunged into work, his waking moments had been dogged by thoughts of her, and when he'd slept—if he'd slept—she'd haunted his dreams, too. He'd woken sweating, frustrated, and more than once to embarrassingly sticky sheets after the dreams had felt vividly, erotically real.

Hot, too, was his shame, seething like a nest of vipers in his belly.

To have treated Lily as he had—a woman effectively under his protection—simply because she'd had the temerity to accuse him of feeling no guilt... How could she have known it was carved across his heart? Touching a wound so raw he'd lashed out, wanting to humble her. A female less than half his size, injured and in pain.

May God forgive him.

But even that wasn't the worst of it. That was not the memory that made his skin crawl with utter self-loathing. He'd saved that for the final tawdry act...the most shaming thing of all.

When he'd confessed his darkest secret she hadn't turned away in revulsion. She'd offered him compassion and comfort. And how had he responded? By almost ravishing her on his desk.

No matter that she'd been eager beneath him, her hands tugging at his clothes. He had known the risks, what might have happened if George had discovered them together. Thank goodness for Sabir's interruption—because even now... Hell, he wasn't sure he'd have stopped without it.

*Yeah, searing, gut-wrenching shame.*

They'd reached his office. The aide pointed out

a number of files awaiting his attention. There was an hour's work there before he retired if he chose.

He ran a palm across his face. When had he last truly rested? Slept for more than a few hours at a time? Sometimes he felt it had been years. But heading to bed with the promise of another night of disturbing dreams did not appeal. He welcomed the prospect of a densely worded report to plough through. It might deaden the clamour in his head.

Dismissing the aide, Khaled fired up his laptop and reached for the first file.

An hour later he was down to the last two. An update on the missing charity funds and the continuing negotiations for the terms of his marriage.

No new evidence had been found to implicate George, and Khaled had done as Lily suggested. Made a noise about how the charity funds were being used, praising Hyde-Wallace for his loyalty and his concern for the Nabhani marshlands. For the time being George couldn't hint at malfeasance without arousing suspicions about how he'd gained that knowledge.

Won over by Khaled's successes in New York, the Council of Families had also rallied round. George was losing his leverage. Meaning he needed to be carefully watched. A cornered animal was dangerous and unpredictable.

As for his marriage? Khaled had told his team to get it done or they'd be looking for new employment. It had worked. He now had water rights on acceptable terms, though his prospective father-in-law continued to hinder reform in the region.

Khaled's hope lay in shape of the seventeen-year-old Crown Prince—a moderniser like himself. Eventually he'd hold the power in Qaydar, and in the meantime he'd be taking the boy's sister to be his wife.

Not the woman he truly desired.

Lily.

What would become of her? Would Nate be there for her? He was all she had.

The thought of her being alone in the world tightened a steel band around Khaled's chest.

He hadn't had George's claims investigated. He couldn't risk it. Word would get out.

His absence from the country had lessened press interest in his mother's guest, and they'd leave her alone completely once he announced his marriage plans. No one would dig any deeper, and Lily's fantasy about her parents could stay intact.

Either way, in less than thirty-six hours he was sending her home. He had no business concerning himself any further in her life.

He closed the laptop. He should try for some sleep. There was another packed day ahead of him, and at the end of it his father's party.

The corridors were deserted as he made his way back to the Family Wing. Leaving him with the sensation of being the only human creature in the Royal Court.

Alone.

Despite the countless people around him, the life of a prince was a solitary one. Would his marriage remove this crushing loneliness? He imagined Aisha waiting for him in his bed. Then tortured himself by putting Lily there instead, her glorious hair spread across the pillow, her slender arms lifting in welcome as he eased into her.

He crossed the last quadrangle and arrived at the stairs to the first floor of the Family Wing. From across the courtyard he caught the flicker of the TV screen in the family room. His steps faltered.

It couldn't be…?

No. She'd be asleep. Safe in bed.

He ignored the disappointment that flared in his chest. It was becoming familiar and, like his other regrets, he'd learn to live with it. He'd have to.

At this hour it could only be his father. Since his heart attacks he often suffered bouts of insomnia. Perhaps he'd catch him watching re-runs of a melodramatic Nabhani soap. It had recently become the King's guilty addiction.

Feeling in profound need of his father's company, all at once Khaled changed direction, heading for the family room.


Sleep just wouldn't come. It had been difficult enough for the last four weeks, but tonight it was impossible.

The reason was due back at any moment.

Lily pulled a wrap over her silk camisole and shorts and slipped from her suite, meaning to seek fresher air out on the veranda, but somehow making her way to the family room.

She flopped down on the sofa in front of the TV. Watching something light-hearted might help. Stop her wasting time thinking about Khaled. Because his leaving the country to put thousands of miles between them had made it pretty clear how he felt about her.

His absence had also changed the nature of the press interest in her. There'd been some reports, dredging up stories of her mother's death, but she'd been carefully protected from the worst of it and their interest seemed to have moved on to Khaled's appearance in New York.

In a few hours she'd see him again.

The shiver of excitement hit instantly, but she tamped it down. She'd had nearly a month to practise controlling the stormy emotions the man unleashed in her. Plenty of time to think about how she'd conduct herself when they next met.

She'd decided she was going to be polite, but distant, as if nothing of any note had ever passed between them. She would attend Bassam's party and the next day ask, politely but firmly, to go home.

Being here, and being welcomed as part of this

family, had been wonderful, but at some point she'd have to return to reality.

She wasn't a child any more, enchanted by fairy tales. Princes didn't sweep nameless girls off their feet and put their needs before everything else.

And she'd be fine—really, she would. She'd always looked after herself before. She could do it again.

The TV was tuned to the local news, in English. Before she could switch programmes there was an announcement of the next segment: a repeat of the Crown Prince's speech to the General Assembly of the United Nations.

Khaled's visit to New York had been a resounding success. Everyone in the palace—family and staff—had talked of little else for the last few days, but she'd not seen the speech before, pleading a headache when the family had gathered to watch the broadcast live, cravenly avoiding any coverage since. She hadn't wanted any reminders of the man.

She should change channels now, but her fingers stalled on the remote.

On screen, the General Assembly appeared. The great hall was full to capacity. Millions more would have watched around the world. Waiting to hear a speech from the enigmatic Crown Prince of Nabhan.

An expectant hush descended as all eyes fell

on the heart of that iconic hall: the podium of green marble.

Lily lifted her legs and wrapped her arms tight about them as the camera zoomed in.

Khaled stepped up. His impeccable suit was a sharp dark navy. His tie ice-blue. The white shirt made a stark contrast to his olive skin and haunting grey eyes.

Lily dropped her chin to her knees, curling up tighter.

His deep voice filled the room. The time was now, he said, calling upon the help of the world to build equality and justice for his homeland and beyond. His voice was confident, his message clear. This was Khaled the consummate statesman.

In that darkened room, with only the TV for company as the rest of the palace slept, Lily watched its prince standing alone, winning over the world's most powerful assembly. All the time hiding the terrible burden he bore of guilt and grief. That he'd caused the death of his beloved brother.

She'd bickered with him and snapped at him and caused him endless trouble. She'd railed at him on Nate's behalf when, to Khaled, it must have felt like his most trusted friend had betrayed him. Making him even more alone.

And she hadn't seen it.

She hadn't understood a thing.

Lily's heart thudded once, twice in her chest,

and then paused. A second later she shivered as it began beating in the same steady rhythm as before, though nothing, *nothing* would ever be the same again.

Because now she understood—finally, and with an awful clarity. Being polite and distant wasn't going to work. There'd be no pushing her feelings aside. She'd been fooling herself.

She was already in love.

Completely, hopelessly in love with the Sad Prince.

His own voice greeted him as he approached the family room. Was his father listening to a repeat of his UN speech?

One of the carved double doors stood wide, spilling a glow across the marble floor ahead. The other cast delicate shifting patterns of light through the fretwork panels. They danced across the pale fabric of his shirt as he drew near.

Khaled halted in the shadows as it registered precisely who was listening to his speech. She sat transfixed, watching him deliver the performance of his life.

What was she thinking?

Presidents and prime ministers had called him after he'd left that podium. Pledging their support for his efforts to drive reform in the region. But the only opinion that mattered right now was that of this young woman.

Weeks and oceans of separation had made no difference.

Want slammed into him.

Khaled lifted a hand. His fingers brushed the door's fretwork, tracing the curve of her cheek, the tumble of auburn hair, the bare toes peeking out from beneath her robe.

How beautiful she was—and how forbidden to him.

One step forward and she would see him.

One step back and he could leave unnoticed.

He dropped his hand, and with a strength he hadn't known he possessed he took a step back.

But his shoe scraped against the floor...

There was someone beyond the fretwork of the door. The light from the TV cast patterns across his shirt. Definitely a man. And he was broad of shoulder and tall. Taller than anyone in the palace except Bassam.

But the King wouldn't hover just out of view. He'd come striding in with a breezy greeting, bemoaning her viewing choices, demanding she change channels, making her smile. More than once she'd kept him company in the early hours, watching old movies or re-runs of his favourite soap when neither of them could sleep.

The figure stayed motionless. Watching her.

Not the King. Though just as tall.

*The son.*

'Khaled…'

His name escaped her on a soft exhaled breath. As if her yearning heart had called directly to him. And now she was on her feet, turning towards that shadowy figure.

Love guided her fingers to loosen the knot on her wrap and let it slip from one shoulder. Cool air hit her sensitised skin. Her nipples peaked.

From the corridor came a long, harsh indrawn breath.

Emboldened, she let the wrap slide again, baring both shoulders.

There was a thud as something landed against the door. A set of fingers appeared, curled around its edge, as if a big body was braced against it.

She heard the faintest low groan. Then all was still.

Had he ever seen anything more lovely? Anything he'd wanted more?

How easy to cross the space between them, gather her up and just this once forget all the things he couldn't have, and didn't deserve, and lose himself in her sweetness?

But they would meet tomorrow publicly at the party, amidst George and his spies. For her safety, he needed her to behave as though she detested him.

He emerged from the shadows. Her expression

drew him forward, step after helpless step, until he stood before her.

The light and welcome in her eyes was nearly his undoing. She lifted her hand, placed her palm against his cheek. On tiptoe, she stretched up to kiss his lips. 'Welcome home,' she said.

He fought the driving need to pull her against him and take them both down onto the sofa. Instead he grasped her wrist and pulled her hand from his face.

'It is not your place to welcome me back. This is not your home. I only came to tell you I shall be making arrangements for you to leave straight after my father's party. Four weeks you've been here. You're on the verge of overstaying your welcome, don't you think?'

He didn't wait for her response. He knew the hurt in her big eyes would destroy him. And how could he explain why he'd rejected her without revealing what she was?

So he turned and walked away, raging with longing and regret, and melted into the darkness, wishing he'd never been there at all.

# CHAPTER THIRTEEN

LILY PACED THE veranda outside her rooms, attempting to steady her nerves.

Her evening gown—a chartreuse silk-satin number, and the single most beautiful thing she'd ever worn—whispered across her toes as she walked. Her newly buffed and freshly painted toes.

That afternoon a cadre of hairdressers and beauticians had set up camp in her suite. From the top of her glossy chignon to the soles of her baby-soft feet she'd been primped and preened till she barely recognised the elegant creature they'd created. Even the seamstress had been on hand, to ensure her gown fitted to perfection—the gown Eleanor had insisted she buy the day Khaled had footed the bill.

She should tear it from her body. Go out there clothed in nothing but a bed sheet rather than parade herself wearing anything his money had bought.

But, oh, *this dress…*

From the swirling hem it rose upwards, its heavy silk lovingly skimming her figure and ending just above the swell of her breasts. A drape of fabric slanted from one shoulder to slide provocatively from the other, revealing impossibly tiny shoestring straps. Then came the truly daring part of the design. The dress plunged at the back, to bare her skin almost to the base of her spine.

She made a turn, shivering in excitement as the sultry evening air drifted across her exposed back. She'd never felt so alluring, so utterly feminine.

Well, good.

Tonight she wanted to be a temptress, a goddess, a veritable man-slayer.

Tonight she wanted to be so desirable that a certain crown prince would be clawing the walls with frustration when he discovered she would never, ever allow him to touch her again. Not if he fell to his knees and begged.

Rejection twice over was enough for a girl to get the message. She wouldn't be risking it a third time.

She sashayed through another turn, shakier this time as she remembered just how it felt to be touched by him...as if a melancholy angel had come down and swept her to heaven.

How pitiful—remembering those moments amongst all the other ones, far less pleasant, when he'd been autocratic, a bully.

Oh, she hated him!

For believing Nate could be a thief.

For blowing hot and cold.

For kissing her with such passion that she'd glimpsed paradise even as he'd snatched it away again.

But she would not be like her mother and throw her heart beneath the feet of a man who didn't care. She would keep her head. She'd get through the next twelve hours and then she'd move on with her life.

With perfect timing, her escort for the evening arrived: a major in the British Army, on attachment to the Queen's staff as equerry. They'd met numerous times over the past weeks and got on well. Tonight he would be someone familiar in a daunting gathering, when the family would be occupied with their royal duties.

The Major took his role seriously, keeping her nerves at bay by recounting hilarious tales on their walk to the party. When the nerves threatened to bubble up as they arrived at the reception rooms he leant closer, telling such a terrible joke that she laughed out loud.

Which was how they made their entrance. An enchanting young woman in a gown of green silk, gliding down the stairs, laughing up into the eyes of her dashing escort.

Stiff with disapproval, Khaled watched Lily's arrival. How she clung to her companion, smiling up at him as if he were the moon and stars and every damn thing that lay between.

Jealousy roiled in his gut, so bitter and sharp he could taste it. He knew the Major, even liked the man, but at that moment he'd have happily smashed a fist into his face.

One word pounded over and over in his skull.

*Mine.*

It was that dress, shimmering over her body as she moved. It was enough to scramble any sensible thought he had.

Before she gained the bottom step and disappeared into the crowding guests she flicked a glance around the room. He waited, barely breathing, until she found him.

When she did, she held his gaze, then speared him with a look of such electrifying sensuality he stopped breathing altogether.

Then her lashes lowered and her expression soured, as if his very existence repulsed her. That hit him, no doubt as she'd intended, right where all the sexual promise had gathered.

Another mantra started in his head. *She's going home tomorrow.* He only had to navigate the next few hours, then he'd never have to see Lily Marchant again.

The French Ambassador was speaking to him. Khaled plastered on an interested expression and set himself to being sociable.

For an hour he circulated, keeping a precise distance from her. It wasn't hard. He just looked for a group of fawning males—because, invariably, she was right in the middle of one. When she moved, he moved.

His ploy worked well enough, until fate threw an elderly relative in his way. The old man was so obviously thrilled to have the Prince's attention that

Khaled lingered longer than he ought to have done. Too late, he became aware of a subtle shift around him, of heads turning, conversations pausing.

He looked up and the reason for their interest became clear.

For there Lily stood. Beautiful. Bristling with hostility.

'Good evening, Your Highness,' she said, sinking into an over-deep curtsy.

He marvelled at how she made such a respectful gesture practically drip disdain.

She rose up, haughty as an empress. Her proud chin lifted. Her neck long. He wanted to press his mouth to it and taste every inch.

'A wonderful party…is it not, *sir*?'

More contempt. For 'sir' he heard *Something unpleasant that lurks beneath a rock*. Aware they were surrounded by dozens of avid observers, not least of whom was Hyde-Wallace, he tried to keep the conversation pleasant.

'I'm glad you're enjoying—'

'The French Ambassador was just saying how glorious everything looks tonight,' she said brightly. 'We agreed the florists have excelled themselves.'

'I think my mother—'

'Though of course it's their job. Oh, look. There's his wife! I really must ask where she found that fabulous gown.'

She spun away without so much as a by-your-leave, dragging her escort with her. She didn't give a damn about that woman's gown. She'd moved in exactly the opposite direction.

Over her head, the equerry sent him a pained look, part apology, part sympathy.

Khaled was left to seethe. She'd snubbed him in every way possible. Breaking protocol by speaking to him before he'd addressed her, interrupting him, and then walking away instead of waiting politely for him to move off first.

And as he wrestled with which impertinence to be most offended by she presented him with the final insult: a view of her departing back.

His mouth went dry. From that angle it was as if the dazzling dress had vanished and there was nothing but delicate spine and endless bare flesh. A male guest leant in to hear something she'd said, placing his hand just where the fabric ended and her naked skin began.

Anger, jealousy and desire churned into a lethal cocktail, and a menacing, barely human sound rumbled up from Khaled's chest.

Eleanor arrived beside him. 'I know you two aren't an item any more,' she said. 'But I do hope you haven't said something to upset Lily?'

'*Me* upset *her*?' It took every atom of self-control he possessed to not tell his beloved, interfering mother to go to hell.

'I wouldn't want her evening spoiled. She's been magnificent tonight. Everyone's talking about her.'

Eleanor's gaze rested on Lily. 'Watching her work the room, you'd think she was born to it.'

Khaled snorted. 'It's only one night. Doing it day after day is the real test.'

'Oh, I suspect Lily is a natural. She's charming everyone.'

'Not quite everyone,' he muttered. 'I'm sorry, but I'm required elsewhere. I'm expecting a call. I've made my apologies to Father.'

Her face fell. 'But you've already worked so many hours today.' She placed a hand on his arm. 'Perhaps you could come back later for the firework display? It's supposed to be particularly dramatic this year.'

Not if he could help it. He'd had his fill of drama for one evening.

An hour later, his call concluded, he sat alone in a darkened anteroom. Sprawled on a sofa, head thrown back, he was quietly fuming.

It had been a failed conversation and it was his fault. He'd been distracted and short-tempered when he should have been conciliatory and diplomatic. He hadn't been able to focus. All he'd been able to think of was Lily in that stunning dress. Surrounded by men feasting their unworthy eyes on her, probably having the same lascivious thoughts he was. He couldn't stand it.

He heard the finale of the evening getting under way in the parade ground. Every year local school-children laid on a musical extravaganza for the

King. Massed drums, pipers and scores of dancers performed traditional Nabhani songs. Afterwards fireworks would be set off from barges in the bay, for everyone across the city to enjoy. Guests and staff alike would be crowding into every vantage point, leaving most of the palace deserted.

Thank God for that, at least. He was in no mood for company.

A light step fell in the doorway.

He lifted his head to see a figure slipping into the room. In a shaft of lamplight from the court-yard he caught a flash of green silk and an ex-panse of pale skin.

Beneath his breath, he cursed.

Unaware she had an audience, Lily bent to slip off her shoes, groaning as her bare soles made con-tact with the marble tiles. There was such an erotic quality to the sound Khaled's entire body tightened.

The drumming from the parade ground grew more thunderous, with the pipes picking up in a mesmerising melody, and—heaven help him— she began swaying her luscious behind in time with the rhythm. Her hands joined in, floating upwards. Her spine arched, her head fell back, and she abandoned herself to a sensuous dance that reignited every forbidden fantasy he'd had about this woman.

Another step sounded outside. A heavy tread. Male.

His gaze snapped to the doorway.

*She was meeting someone. Right under his nose. Not in this lifetime.*

Blind jealousy propelled Khaled to his feet and across the room before his rational mind had time to stop him.

A hand across her mouth stifled the scream before Lily could make it. An arm lifted her clean off her feet as she was swept backwards to the rear exit of the room.

She struggled—until a growled, 'Be still!' identified her captor and her fear became righteous anger instead.

She'd slipped away from the party to have a few minutes in which she could stop smiling and pretending that her heart wasn't breaking.

Now the very cause of her misery was right here, hauling her about like a piece of baggage.

Khaled dumped her back on her feet, manacled her wrist with his fingers and set off down the deserted corridor, towing her behind him.

She yanked at her trapped arm. 'Let go of me!'

'No.'

His scowling gaze fixed forward, his robes billowing around him as he walked, he looked every inch the desert prince: proud, vital, and maddeningly handsome.

Lily's heart skipped a beat.

She was weak, weak, *weak*—wanting him even while he was behaving like a tyrant.

At the party she'd searched for him as subtly as she could. Her heart squeezing when she'd spotted his imposing figure, spectacular in his robes, but not by so much as a flicker of recognition had he acknowledged her. It was pride and hurt that had made her send him that smouldering look. When she'd seen desire flare in his eyes she'd deliberately looked away, hoping she'd left him burning with need.

She'd wanted to shake that cool façade.

Then she'd wanted to forget him entirely.

'I'm not going anywhere with you.' She stopped dead.

Without missing a step he carried on, dragging her with him. She only just kept her feet.

Through empty corridors they went. Across courtyards echoing to the thunder of fireworks as the display began. Past placid pools reflecting the starbursts overhead. Into the Family Wing he marched her, then up the stairs, and along the veranda, with its romantic lanterns and vista of lush trees below. He ignored it all, only stopping when they arrived at her suite. He pulled her inside it, kicking the door shut behind them, before finally throwing her arm from him in disgust.

Lily rubbed at her wrist while he prowled back and forth, his furious stare fixed on her bedroom, where the lamps were lit and the bed turned down ready for her return.

'So what have I done this time?' she snapped.

He turned towards her.

'You flaunt yourself all evening. Treat me with blatant disrespect. And then dare ask how you have transgressed?'

Flaunt herself? She'd quit the party to get *away* from male attention.

She stamped her foot in frustration. There was a soft slapping sound. She'd left her shoes behind.

He snorted. 'Bare feet, green dress, bad behaviour. All we need now is something for you to steal and we'll be back where we started.'

She glared at him. 'You're despicable.'

'I'm merely stating facts.'

'Facts? The facts are that I did nothing but try to be pleasant to your father's guests. I smiled. I chatted. I attempted to be charming. You should try it sometimes. It'd be a big improvement on how you normally conduct yourself.'

That landed a blow.

His cheekbones flared red. 'You'll curb that insolent tongue—or, so help me, I will take you across my knee.'

'You could try,' she flung back at him.

'Do not challenge me.' He took a step closer.

'Then don't threaten me.' She stepped nearer, too.

His eyes, diamond-hard, glittered down on her. 'Have a care,' he cautioned, 'and remember who you're speaking to.'

'Oh, I'm sorry.' She dipped into her second mocking curtsy of the night. 'God forbid that anyone should point out when you're behaving badly, Your High and Mightiness.'

He moved lightning-fast, grabbing her waist, hauling her against him. 'Damn it. You will show me some respect.'

'I'll do that when you behave in a manner that earns it,' she snapped.

His eyes flashed. He was breathing hard. His whole body vibrated with anger.

'Woman,' he growled, 'this time you go too far.'

And his mouth crashed down on hers.

Oh, no. He was not going to drag her about, accuse her of being a shameless flirt, and then expect to kiss her into submission.

She struggled against him and the onslaught of his lips. 'No! You didn't want me last night. Now I don't want you.'

He lifted his head, shot a tormented glance at her bed. When he looked back his expression was one of raw need.

'Lily…' he groaned. 'For the love of God. Kiss me.'

That plea was her undoing. That and the hunger in his eyes, practically eating her alive.

He wasn't trying to punish her. He wanted her.

Everything soft and feminine in her responded. Her own need burst into life inside her. Her breasts ached. Her nipples peaked. Between her legs she was damp.

Realisation dawned. Last night he'd rejected

her not because he didn't want her, but because he wouldn't allow himself to have her, to be happy.

Her hands lifted, ripping the *thurgal* and the white *ghutrah* from his head. She plunged her fingers into his hair. His mouth covered hers again, then moved lower, along her throat, her collarbone. Licking, nipping, teasing, right to the swell of her breast.

In ecstasy, she arched against him. Her dress slipped to her waist. He'd lowered the zip. When? How? She'd felt nothing but the blazing delight of his mouth and fingers moving over her skin.

The stunning dress fell from her hips to pool at their feet. He lifted her clear, his mouth back on hers. Her naked breasts, belly, thighs…all were crushed against him.

A small, quiet voice urged caution, but it was too late. She was lost to reason. She let him carry her to the bed. Tumble them both onto it.

Desperate to touch him, she pushed the gauzy black *bisht* off his shoulders and began wrestling with the buttons of his *dishdasha*. He simply dragged everything over his head, flinging it all to the floor in a wild tangle. He disposed of his shoes and underwear, then stretched out over her.

He was stunning. Golden-skinned, exquisitely muscled…

Lily blinked.

*Big*.

The glide of his hands distracted her, slipping

beneath her behind, lifting her clear of the bed so he could ease her knickers down her legs. He tossed them aside.

Panting in little staccato breaths, she squirmed as his hot gaze roved her naked body.

'Beautiful,' he breathed, sliding a hand to her thigh, lifting it, opening her up to him.

With a flex of his hips he pushed into her.

Lily cried out.

It hurt.

She was shocked at how much.

Startled understanding flared in his eyes. He knew now that she had lied about her experience.

He began easing back.

'No, don't stop…make love to me… Khaled, please.' The words tumbled out as she lifted her hips, offering herself to him, dragging his head down to hers, kissing him over and over.

'Not like this. I'll hurt you,' he said roughly against her mouth.

'I don't care.'

'But I do.' He captured a hand and planted a kiss in her palm. '*Habiba*, hush. I'm not going anywhere. But we're going to take this slowly.'

He swept a tangle of hair from her brow and placed his lips there instead, then over her eyes, across her cheek, soothing her, calming her. He found the tender spot beneath her ear and sucked softly. She shuddered as lust surged through her.

His head went lower and his mouth fastened on

her breast, taking a nipple between his teeth. He bit down and Lily moaned.

Warm hands floated along her flank, over her belly then one slid between her thighs.

A gentle exploration at first. Delicate, enticing.

Not enough. She moved against him. A finger slid inside her, then a second, moving gently back and forth until she was slick and juicy and grinding shamelessly into the heel of his hand.

Suddenly his fingers were gone, and in one swift movement he was inside her.

The sharp pain stole her breath, but he held absolutely still, giving her time to adjust to his body inside hers.

'Okay?'

The look of tender concern melted her heart. She nodded.

He withdrew, then eased himself back into her. And waited.

The tightly corded muscles of his neck told her what this restraint was costing him. But the ache had lessened and the feeling of fullness was... good.

He thrust again. Deeper.

The ache was giving way to a new raft of sensations.

Little tremors racked her as he increased the pace. Waves of pleasure that ebbed and flowed and built higher with every pass of his body inside hers. His hands caressed her, held her, guided her. And his mouth…oh, the glory of his mouth. Against her own, at her neck, on her breasts. She whimpered and sighed and moaned as he took her higher and higher.

She sensed him losing control and loved it. Loved watching his face twist in sweet anguish as pleasure ripped through him, too. Loved how his movements became more urgent, how his fingers curled through hers and clung on. And the storm in his eyes as he held her gaze sent her heart soaring.

All the pain of rejection became meaningless, sunk beneath the wondrous knowledge that she'd brought him to this. To the soul-wrenching groan and the spurt of heat low in her belly as he poured himself into her.

And that was when bright, blinding pleasure overtook her.

On a long, keening cry, Lily threw back her head and convulsed around him.

Khaled lay there, shaken, his heart thundering wildly in his chest. He'd never been like that before at the end. So out of control.

'*Habiba?*' He raised his head. 'I'm sorry. Did I hurt you?'

She brushed her knuckles across his cheek. 'It's okay. I'm good.'

He leant into that caress, felt her forgiveness pouring balm over this new guilt, and deep inside a fissure appeared in that older knot of self-loathing.

She began wriggling, squirming to get out from beneath him. He lifted himself up. Let her push him on to his back. Then she knelt beside him, staring at his torso and his sex as if she wanted to devour him. He'd let her.

She moved over him, her glorious hair trailing like silk over his shoulder. She pressed her lips to his collarbone, across his sternum, then took a tight nipple between her teeth.

He groaned. She kissed the little hurt she'd made and sent him the smile of a courtesan.

His fists clenched in the sheets.

This was pure madness.

Wrong to have dragged her back to this room.

Even worse to stay. He should leave now. But he could no more do that than tell his heart to cease beating.

She went lower, over his abdomen, using her lips and her tongue to explore each ridge of muscle with tormenting thoroughness. Finally, with a hum of pleasure, she took him into her mouth, tasting them both with a sweep of her tongue that sent his hands into her hair.

Her eyes held his as she worked him. Learning how to please him. Teasing him, testing him. Driving him to the edge of sanity. He stopped her before he lost the power to control anything. She sent him that smile again and, as if she'd been sa-vouring a feast, licked her lips.

The minx.

Well, two could play at that game.

He rolled on top of her, pinning her down, kiss-ing her breasts, nuzzling the soft flesh, lapping at each distended nipple. Excited by her moans of pleasure, he kissed lower and lower, to the curls between her thighs.

She was honey-sweet. Like nothing he'd ever tasted. He couldn't get enough. He kissed, he licked, he suckled the little bud at the very heart of her.

She bucked and writhed but he held her down with a hand splayed across her belly. Watching her come apart, hearing her broken little cries, was the most erotic thing he'd ever witnessed. Oh, how he wanted this woman.

He rose to his knees, grasped her hips and shoved into her, groaning as the last of her or-gasm pulsed around him.

She'd been a virgin. He should be more gentle. But he couldn't. He'd never known such abandon.

A wild joy leapt in his chest. *Mine*, he thought, fiercely. *Truly mine.* Something pure and good. Completely untainted by years of self-loathing.

That new fissure cracked wider.

He thrust again, and Lily arched beneath him on a long sigh of bliss. With a smile—a dazzling sunshine smile she'd never gifted him before—

she placed her hand on his chest, over his heart, and lifted her hips. Giving herself to him so completely he felt that cold, unyielding part of him finally shatter into pieces and knew he was changed for ever.

*Love*, he thought, half dazed. *It's love. I love her.*

Trembling now, he lay over her, crushing her into the mattress, desperate to imprint himself on every inch of her. His sweat bathed her body, his seed was in her mouth and in her womb, but it wasn't enough. He wanted to be the very air she breathed. He wanted to be lodged indelibly in her heart. He wanted her as changed as he was.

'Lily…' he breathed. Like a vow.

Then he sealed her lips with his and set about seducing her all over again.

Her hands dug into his buttocks, pulling him in closer. Her hips rose up to meet his. 'More,' she moaned, urging him on.

And all finesse forgotten, pumping hard and fast, he answered that siren call. Utterly lost in her.

# CHAPTER FOURTEEN

THE STEADY *THUMP-THUMP* against her ear was soothing. Khaled's heartbeat, and the slow fall and rise of his chest as he slept, was not what woke her. That was the far-off whir of a helicopter, ferrying away the last of the party guests.

The noise disappeared into the night and Lily nestled closer. Khaled's arms enclosed her, his chin rested on top of her head. Whatever came next could wait until tomorrow. For now, she was cocooned in happiness.

She pressed her lips to his chest, laid her cheek on that same spot, and drifted back to sleep.

When she woke again the noise was closer. This time from outside her rooms. Someone was at the door.

She stirred in Khaled's arms, about to wake him.

'It's all right. I hear it.' He pushed up to an elbow as another knock sounded, more urgent.

'Put on your wrap,' he whispered, 'and go and see who it is.'

In the sitting room, she scooped up his *ghutrah* and black *agal* and tucked them away from view. Her discarded dress she laid neatly over the sofa, as if removed when she undressed herself, not stripped away by the hands of a lover.

She was no fool. The Prince being found in her rooms would be scandalous.

She ran her hands through her tangled hair, tightened her wrap, then cracked open the door.

On the other side, his expression grave, stood Sabir.

'Miss Marchant, forgive me. I must urgently find His Highness.'

Should she to lie to his secretary? 'He's… He's…'

'Here.'

Khaled emerged from the bedroom, almost dressed, pulling on the gauzy black *bisht*, his face just as shadowed. 'What is it?'

The secretary entered the suite, quietly closing the door behind him.

'Sir, it's your father. He collapsed in his rooms twenty minutes ago.'

Lily gasped, her face lifting to Khaled's.

A muscle flexed in his jaw. 'How bad is it?'

'The doctors don't know yet, sir. He's being helicoptered to hospital. The Queen is with him.'

The noise Lily had heard. Not the departure of happy guests but Bassam, that kind, wonderful man, being rushed to Emergency.

'Your mother asks that you follow with the Princesses,' Sabir said.

Eleanor was gathering the family. She must fear the worst. Lily's heart ached for them. And for the man beside her most of all, with that terrible new fear in his eyes.

'How can I help?' She laid a hand on his arm. 'Shall I come with you? I could be with the girls?'

'No, it wouldn't be appropriate.' He dismissed her offer without a glance, but then, on a shuddering breath, snatched her close, kissing her brow, softening the blow. 'But thank you for your kindness. Stay here. I'll send someone to you later. There are things between us to discuss.'

He offered only that cryptic comment. So she pressed her hands to his chest, giving comfort in the only way she could.

Until he was gone, striding away, and Sabir, with a bow, closed the door after them.

It was three in the morning—hours before the palace would be up—but going back to sleep would be impossible.

Lily perched on her bed and slid a hand into the tangle of sheets. Still warm from their bodies. Hers melted at the memory of what they'd done together, how he'd unravelled for her.

*There are things between us to discuss.*

A stunning notion had her on her feet, pacing the room. Was she seriously imagining Khaled might propose to her? How wrong to be thinking of her own happiness when Bassam might be fighting for his life. But she couldn't help it. Last night had changed everything.

Khaled kept everyone at a distance. Even his family. He'd woven a near impenetrable barrier about himself. But when he'd sunk into her that final time there had been such a fragile joy in his eyes she'd known he'd surrendered an essential piece of himself to her.

For now, she'd wait as asked, and pray that Bassam would recover.

She showered, dressed, set her suite to rights. A servant normally did this, but today she resorted to housekeeper mode, needing to be busy.

She found a TV documentary about the Nabhani coastline. Two hours passed during which she stared at a screen filled with dolphins and whale sharks and took in almost nothing.

The sky lightened and early-morning sunshine poured in through her windows, filling the room with a brightness and hope she desperately clung to. A teary-eyed servant arrived with a breakfast tray, but no news.

The palace staff were waiting. Like her.

She nibbled on fruit, sipped tea, but had no real appetite. She was too worried for Khaled, desperate to be with him, to comfort him, support him.

Beneath a cushion she spied his neatly folded *ghutrah*. She drew it out and lifted it to her cheek, inhaling its beloved hint of citrus and spice.

She must have dozed, because suddenly she was jerking upright as the phone in her suite rang.

'I see the Prince hasn't given you up.'

Waking from dreams of Khaled, the unexpected voice confused her.

'Excuse me?'

'Don't bother denying it,' said George Hyde-Wallace. 'I know he spent the night rutting in your bed. But you should know he can't marry you.'

She fought off the remnants of sleep.

'As Leader of the Council of Families, when I see our future king being beguiled by an unsuitable woman, I must act.'

Unsuitable? That woke her up. 'I'm the granddaughter of a duke.'

'Biological granddaughter only, I'm afraid. Your father didn't bother to check that his wedding was legal. He wasn't married in the eyes of the law, which makes you illegitimate—and so barred from ever being our Queen. In short, you are entirely ineligible.'

Shock silenced her. That cherished image of her father, the fact that he'd loved her mother enough to whisk her away to a tropical beach for their ceremony. Was even that a lie?

'Imagine the scandal,' George drawled. 'The great name of Azir being linked with a woman of questionable birth. There would be a constitutional crisis. It might even destroy the monarchy. But you can prevent that if you do as I say.'

She wanted to denounce him for the scheming traitor he was, but she had to think of Khaled and his family.

'What do you want me to do?'

'The King may not last the day, and by nightfall your lover might be our new monarch.'

*Oh, Bassam.* Lily squeezed her eyes shut against the sting of tears.

'There must be no hint of scandal…of anything that might throw a shadow on the Prince taking the throne. If you leave now, I'll make sure what I've discovered never reaches the press. A car will be on the palace forecourt in ten minutes to take you to the airport. You have a seat booked on the next flight to London. Be on it.'

Whatever rosy future she'd hoped for, she knew she had to walk away and spare the royal family the trauma of a scandal. Even if that meant never seeing Khaled again.

Somehow keeping the heartbreak out of her voice, she said, 'Okay, I'll do it.'

'A wise decision. Let's just say a foreign national getting caught up in all this would be… inconvenient.'

There was no chance for her to ask what that meant. George had cut the connection.

Numb with shock, Lily replaced the receiver, then realised she still held Khaled's *ghutrah*, crushed in her other hand. The once crisp white cotton was crumpled and soiled. Now it was no better than a rag.

No longer fit for a prince.

She had only ten minutes before that car arrived, and she was grateful. Less time to dwell on what she'd just learned. She focused instead on preparing to leave.

She was already dressed in jeans and a T-shirt. While Khaled had been in the States her bank card had been returned, and her passport delivered from London. She tucked them into her back pocket now. She grabbed a sweater for the plane, a jacket for travelling through London, and she was ready.

Everything else she left. Including the dress she'd first arrived in. She'd never wear it again. The memories would be too painful. Even the clothes now on her back she'd donate to a women's refuge. She wanted no reminders of her time here.

She sat down to pen a note to Eleanor, thanking her for all her kindness and explaining why she'd had to leave so suddenly. Something about it being too uncomfortable for her now Khaled was home again and wanting to give the family space while the King was ill…

It wasn't entirely untrue.

She looked up at the knock on her door. Time to leave already? Her stomach twisted.

But it was Sabir, and all other thoughts fled as she took in the secretary's anxious expression.

'No, madam, please do not upset yourself,' Sabir quickly reassured her. 'His Majesty is still poorly but doing better than expected. The doctors think he over-exerted himself at the party. He danced with the schoolchildren…' He gave a small smile. 'He did not want to disappoint them. It's a tradition that he does so every year.'

She slumped in relief. 'Is the family still with him?'

'Yes, madam.'

'And the Prince?' she asked tentatively. 'How is he?'

'He is naturally much relieved.' Sabir suddenly looked discomforted. 'But he has sent me to talk to you. May I come in?'

*There are things between us to discuss.*

Whatever they were made little difference now. Even if Khaled had been thinking of proposing to her she couldn't accept.

Lily walked back to the sofas and sat down, gesturing to the one opposite hers. He followed her and sank down, looking deeply troubled. Nothing like the normally calm Sabir.

'His Highness has first asked me to convey to you the extremely high regard in which he holds you,' he began. 'How in the short time since you have been reacquainted you have come to mean a great deal to him.' He paused, his hands working nervously around the leather binder he carried. 'But he regrets that he is unable to make you any formal offer. Instead he has an alternative arrangement.'

A 'formal offer' being a proposal of marriage? Here she was, about to make the grand gesture and sacrifice her happiness to keep him safe, and he wasn't about to offer his hand anyway.

The last of Lily's hopes withered around her.

'A private jet is standing by to take you to Greece,' Sabir said. 'His Highness has a villa on an island there which from now on will be permanently at your disposal. He will join you when he can, though at the moment he can't say when that will be. In the longer term, should you wish it, a property may be organised elsewhere, providing it is discreet and within easy distance of his usual travel routes. It cannot, of course, be in Nabhan.'

Sabir opened the binder and withdrew a sheet of paper, placing it on the coffee table between them.

'In addition to the property, this is the sum that will be settled on you per annum.'

She tried to make sense of the astonishing figure. More each year than she could hope to earn in a lifetime.

'He was most insistent that I make it clear you will want for nothing ever again.'

Except her self-respect.

Beyond Sabir, the door to her bedroom stood open—the room where Khaled had made love to her as if she were precious to him. Say yes and she'd see him, touch him, be held by him again. If there was no marriage who'd care that she was illegitimate? George's threats had become meaningless.

For a heartbreaking few seconds she actually

considered it. Sacrificing everything to take the life he offered her.

*But what life?* a stark voice asked her.

Because she knew exactly what his offer meant.

Never again would she hold her head up and walk through the palace, sit with Eleanor and the twins in her sunny sitting room or keep Bassam company in the wee small hours when neither of them could sleep.

As for seeing Khaled… It would be like last night. Snatched moments, secret assignations. A life lived in the shadows. Never would she be publicly acknowledged, but everyone would know what she was, and behind her back they would call her by that name.

*Mistress.*

Or, worse.

Because she'd be complicit in making Khaled an adulterer, his new wife cheated on from the start. That poor woman…

And where would she truly be in his list of priorities? After his wife, after his family, after his country? He wasn't even choosing her second, and when he tired of her, and the difficulties of conducting such a relationship, what then? There'd be a pay-off—generous, no doubt—but she would be permanently dropped from his life. To do what? With the only skills on her CV earned while lying on her back?

She was her mother's daughter after all. Giving her heart to a man only to discover she wasn't that important to him. Because if she were Khaled would never have offered something that served his needs entirely at the expense of hers.

There had been no surrender last night. At least not from him. He'd just been sampling the wares to see if they would suit his purpose. Taking her to bed with no thought of the consequences for her.

*Consequences?* Lily's stomach flipped. They hadn't used any kind of protection. She hadn't given it a moment's thought. Her hand went reflexively to her belly.

'And if…if there were any children?'

Sabir looked even more uncomfortable.

'Sadly, they could not be publicly recognised, but they would know their father.'

No, they would not. She would not be a party to that. Hiding sweet, blameless babies away like dirty little secrets. No matter how much she loved their father.

She buried her face in her hands as a wave of something like grief tore through her. Was this how her mother had felt? Was it this agony that had made her give up on life and drink herself to death?

But she was not her mother. She was stronger. She could survive on her own and she was definitely worth more than a life lived skulking in secret.

She'd decline Khaled's shameful offer because Lily Marchant was done with being second-best.

She lifted her head. 'The flight to Greece—can it be rearranged to take me home to London, instead?'

Sabir's expression brightened. 'Yes, Miss Marchant. It can.'

'And how soon can I leave?'

'As soon as you wish it.' He stood, purposeful and efficient Sabir again. 'I'll make the arrangements at once.'

'You won't get into trouble?'

He sent her a rueful look. 'You must let me worry about that, madam.' He was at the door when he turned back to her. 'This recent offer notwithstanding, His Highness is a good man.'

She gazed up at him. 'I'm going to miss you, Sabir.'

'And I shall miss you, and how the Prince has been with you here.'

Her mouth lifted in a small, sad smile. 'Impossible, you mean?'

'No, madam. Alive. More alive than I have ever seen him.'

A lump of raw anguish knotted her throat. 'Look after him for me, won't you?' she whispered.

Nonsensical though that was, Sabir, bless him, answered as if it mattered. 'Always. You have my word on it.'

With that he gave her a low bow that she'd only ever seen him use with the King and Queen. The highest mark of respect he could bestow upon her. And that little kindness helped bolster her resolve more than he knew, because as he left, taking with him her last link to his master, and her world turned empty and grey, she almost ran after him, to tell him she'd changed her mind. But that bow reminded her that to some she was worthy of respect. Worthy of more than a life lived as man's plaything. However exalted the man himself might be.

Khaled's royal head gear still sat on the sofa beside her. The crumpled white cloth and the roped circlet taunted her. To think a few hours ago she'd imagined their owner might be about to make her his princess! What planet had she been living on?

She stood, leaving them where they lay. They were meaningless to her now.

George's promised car would be waiting.

Let it. She was leaving anyway. What did it matter how? He had spies who'd informed him that she and Khaled had been together last night. Let him find out she'd left in the same underhand way.

She wandered to the window, to gaze one last time at the dazzling view—another thing she knew would haunt her dreams in the years to come—and to wait for Sabir's call.

It took her a few seconds to register that the soldiers patrolling the dunes today were much closer than usual. Almost in the palace grounds. Several of them were moving together and crouched low. That wasn't normal either. Was this an exercise?

Icy fingers crawled along at Lily's spine. The men were masked, their weapons raised.

What had George said? A foreign national getting caught up in this would be inconvenient? Was this what he'd meant? Was he launching an attack on the palace itself?

The security in this part of the Family Wing was minimal, to allow everyone their privacy. If they'd already got past the perimeter guards, how easily might those men below reach the Royal Court itself?

In the next breath, Lily was sprinting along the veranda. She had to warn Sabir and the rest of the staff.

At the entrance lobby, she skidded to a halt. Two of the men were already inside, creeping from the direction of the garden. Behind them was a third figure, taller, leaner, but as intimidating as the mercenaries, in head-to-toe black combat gear. He pulled off his mask as he saw her.

George Hyde-Wallace was brazen enough to join the attack himself.

'Still here?' he said. 'How tiresome you Marchants are. Always getting in the way.'

His thugs aimed their weapons at her chest. Lily froze, trying to control her terror and *think*.

'If only he'd given you up and married Aisha, as I wanted. You'd have been spared this.' He stalked towards her. 'Too late now. Your fate is tied to his.'

The rattle of gunfire sounded from the Royal Court. Lily's heart almost stopped.

'Yes. You're witnessing a coup,' George said, almost casually. 'At this moment my men are at the hospital, removing your lover and his family from power. In the next hour they'll be on a flight out and heading into exile.'

Exile. Not execution. It was a sliver of hope amidst the horror. Khaled might survive this.

'You'd betray the family and the country that have given you everything?' she said. 'You're disgusting.'

George lashed out so fast there was no time to flinch. The back of his hand smashed into her cheek and sent her sprawling sideways. Her head caught on a side table as she went down. Pain exploded in her temple...the coppery tang of blood spilled over her lips.

He grabbed her shoulders and hauled her to her knees, pushing his face into hers. 'And you are nothing but a common harlot,' he snarled.

Through the agony in her jaw, the near-paralysing fear and the raw ache in her heart, she summoned what courage she had to lift her head and face him. 'Better a harlot than a filthy traitor.'

He flung her from him as if she was something foul he'd been obliged to touch. 'I wonder how the Prince could bear to entangle himself with you. Being aware of the stain you would be on his family.'

A new anguish tore at her. Khaled knew about her parents…?

'Oh, didn't I mention it?' George said with a reptilian smile. 'I told him before he left for America. Why do you think he departed so suddenly?'

Because he'd discovered she was only good enough to warm his bed and hadn't even cared enough to explain why.

Lily's heart cracked wide open.

There was a shout from behind them and a lone figure appeared at the entrance to the Royal Court.

A man supposed to be on his way to a life of exile.

But instead there he stood, like an avenging angel. More beautiful than she'd ever seen him and never more out of reach.

'Azir…' George hissed, and a lifetime of loathing was crammed into that name.

'As you see,' Khaled said.

His ice-cold gaze raked the scene: Lily crumpled on the floor, bloody and bruised, George towering over her.

'Your plot has failed and you're finished—but touch the woman again and you'll die where you stand.'

George's face turned puce and veins bulged in

his forehead. In a flash of movement he whipped a revolver from his belt, hauled Lily upwards, and jammed the gun into her bruised temple.

'You want the whore?' he said, clamping his other hand around her throat. 'Well, come and get her.'

His two mercenaries drew in beside him. Like George, they were using Lily's body as cover.

'It's over, man,' Khaled said quietly. 'You've nowhere to go. Think of your wife. Think of your sons.'

George stepped back, dragging Lily with him. 'My sons? They were too afraid to be a part of this. What use are they to me now?'

Khaled matched his every step. Talking all the while as Rais and his men fanned out, cutting off any escape route.

'Your sons aren't here because they're ashamed of you and what you've become. They're the ones who called to warn me of your attack.'

There was a low, menacing growl from the man beside her. She wanted to scream at Khaled to stop. Stop baiting him. But the fingers wrapped around her throat had tightened. All she could do was watch in horror as Khaled came closer.

Then her hip glanced off another side table. She remembered there was a vase of flowers on it. She stretched out, groping for it. Her fingers found the rim and she heaved it upwards, aiming at George's head. It was only a glancing blow, but the drench of cold water and the falling stems covering them both loosened his grip just enough for her to wrench free.

She had split seconds while George pushed sodden hair from his eyes. She couldn't hope to wrestle his gun away or to disarm his two guards. She had one thing. The protection of her body.

Praying that her shaking legs would support her, Lily took off. Aiming straight for Khaled.

He bellowed at her to get down. When she was two paces out he sidestepped, moving to snatch her to safety behind him.

*No.*

She launched herself straight at his chest.

Their eyes locked. In his was such a hollowed-out terror she almost believed he cared for her. But not enough to put her needs first, to be honest with her and let her go.

Her heart shattered all over again just as two pistol shots sounded behind her.

Something slammed into her back. Hard. The extra momentum was enough to send Khaled flailing backwards, and her body went down with him.

There was the rattle of automatic weapons, and strangled cries as booted feet pounded by.

Urgent hands turned her onto her side, pressed against her back. A voice yelled her name over and over, begging her to stay with him.

Stay with him?

'Why? You don't really want me,' she said out loud…or perhaps not. It was getting harder to breathe and, though she tried, she couldn't keep her eyes open.

George must have hit her harder than she'd thought. Her mouth was filling with blood and everything else was blurred, coming from further and further away.

At last only one thing punctured the gathering gloom: an unearthly, inhuman roar sounding next to her, like an animal in unspeakable pain.

Then there was nothing but the quiet and the dark and Lily, unbearably weary and sad, gave herself up to it.

# CHAPTER FIFTEEN

THERE WAS A drift of voices. Lily tried to focus. Was she awake or dreaming? It was so hard to tell.

'Sir, you cannot remain in this room all the time. The patient is in my care and I must insist you leave.'

A woman was speaking. There was an indefinable accent to her English, but no mistaking the determined tone.

'Come on, mate. It's been nearly three days.'

This from a man, gently cajoling.

'The Sister is right. It won't hurt to step out for a while.'

'I will not.'

The third voice—also male, but not in the least conciliatory—sent a ripple of unease through Lily. Who was he that she should be afraid of him?

'I have to be here when she wakes.'

Now he sounded desperate.

'I have to be, Nate.'

*Nate.*

Her head felt stuffed with cotton wool, her body equally feeble, but Lily summoned what strength she had and forced her eyelids open.

Three figures swam into view.

Nate was here. Whoever that other man was, she was safe.

Perhaps she'd given voice to that fervent wish. Three heads swivelled in her direction.

'Baby Sis? Oh, thank God.'

Nate reached her side and took her hand. The woman, a nurse in spotless scrubs, bustled towards her, smiling kindly. The third figure, the owner of that disturbing voice, came closer, too, but Lily instinctively shrank back. A bolt of pain shot through her right side.

'Where am I?' Her voice was a scrape of air in her throat.

'You're in the Prince Faisal Hospital. You were injured, but you're safe now,' Nate said, squeezing her hand.

The nurse fussed around her, checking tubes and charts.

'Injured?'

'There was an attack on the palace,' the stranger said. That voice… It was so achingly familiar… Who *was* he?

The memory hovered, just out of reach.

She'd been running. To warn someone.

Her gaze focused on Nate.

'Sabir? The staff?'

It wasn't Nate who answered.

'They're all safe, *habiba*.'

*Sweetheart.*

Fragments of memory formed.

There had been a night. A magical night when, out of love, she'd given herself to a man. She glanced at him. *This man.* He'd called her sweetheart. His big body had moved over her, inside her, coaxing her to the heights of ecstasy and she'd given him everything she was.

But what had she been worth to him? The position of mistress. Good enough to warm his bed. But nothing more.

Second-best.

The hurt and humiliation came flooding back.

She tugged her stepbrother closer. 'I don't want him here.'

Khaled flinched as if he'd been struck. 'Lily, let me explain.'

Frowning, the Sister planted herself firmly between him and her patient. He turned ashen, as if he couldn't quite believe what was happening.

'Come, now,' said Nate. 'I know he can be a difficult bugger, but does he really deserve to be sent out, hmm?'

Lily tightened her grip on his hand. *'Please.'*

Nate searched her face and finally, exhaling heavily, turned to the other man. 'I'm sorry, mate, but perhaps you'd better give us a moment.'

At first it looked as if Khaled would refuse. The muscles in his jaw working, he stared at Nate. But then, with a last anguished look at Lily, he spun away and left the room.

She crumpled in relief.

'Baby Sis, what the hell's going on?'

'Oh, Nate,' she wailed, 'I've been such a fool.'

* * *

The requested 'moment' stretched into four long, tortuous days. Days when Khaled thought he might actually lose his mind.

He'd barely kept it together during those terrible hours after the shooting, in the agonising wait while Lily was in surgery to remove two bullets. She'd taken one to the shoulder; another had collapsed her lung. Later, while she lay unconscious, he'd sat with her, holding her hand, willing her to come back to him.

But this waiting was a whole new level of torment.

She was recovering well, her doctors said. She was young and strong and responding to treatment as they would wish. There would be no lasting damage.

Physically.

Her state of mind was another matter. After what she'd been through that would take longer to be restored. His Highness would need to be patient.

Patient? He was practically wearing a hole in the floor outside her room.

Lily was being cared for in the same private wing of the hospital where his father was recuperating. After refusing point-blank to leave, Khaled had been given an adjacent guest suite, complete with office facilities. But he was barely in it. Sleep was fleeting. Neither could he work. Nothing held his focus.

Right now, all he cared about in the world was on the other side of that closed door.

And refusing to have anything to do with him.

Could he blame her? Hadn't he done the same as all those who'd gone before? Put her needs second to his with that shameful offer he could hardly bear to think of now.

The truth was, he'd panicked. With his father perhaps on his deathbed, and his enemies closing in, a dynastic marriage had seemed his only option. And taking Lily as his mistress had seemed the only way to keep her in his life.

What did he have now?

In his most desolate moments, may God forgive him, he'd been glad they'd been so careless as to make love without protection. She'd be irrevocably bound to him if she carried his child.

After being told she did not, he'd felt as if she were slipping even further away. As lost to him as if she'd died at his feet on the palace floor. Like Faisal. Gone for good.

How was he to bear it?

Nate remained the only visitor she'd see. He'd dashed from the marshes as soon as he'd heard Lily had been injured. Hours later had come news about the theft. The real culprit was unmasked. Had confessed, actually.

Lily had been right all along. The secretary was responsible. Penny had been secretly in love with George since she'd worked for him years earlier, and the bastard had played on that, persuading her to do his dirty work.

After the attempted coup, Penny had come to her senses and walked into a police station to confess all.

She'd done it for love, she'd said. The same reason Lily had thrown herself between a prince and his would-be assassin. Even though she'd believed her love wasn't reciprocated.

*'You don't really want me.'*

Those barely whispered words as she'd lain bleeding in his arms had been a lance through his heart. Would he ever get the chance to put things right?

For now, he'd done everything it was in his power to do. All that was left to him was to watch the back and forth of her medical staff—and wait.

On the afternoon of the fourth day the doctors pronounced her to be progressing well enough to go home and continue her convalescence there.

Home? Khaled thought, slumped in a chair. Where was that to be?

'Khaled, mate.'

He looked up. Nate stood beside him.

'She wants to see you.'

He was out of his seat and halfway to her room before a firm hand to his shoulder stopped him.

'Wait. I need to say something. I know you love her. I've never seen you like this before. And I'm pretty sure she feels the same way. But whatever you did, I don't think she's forgiven you yet. If you can persuade her otherwise, you have my blessing. But I give you fair warning: hurt her again and I'll shoot you myself.'

He wouldn't argue with that. When the time came, would he demand anything less of those courting Amal or Hanan?

The last hurdle was the Sister, standing sentinel on the threshold, watching his approach with undisguised disapproval. 'We're right outside if she needs us,' she warned him, before reluctantly letting him pass and closing the door behind him.

The afternoon sun glinted towards him, gilding two armchairs set by the window. In one of them, dressed in a satin robe, her hair falling loose about her shoulders, a blanket over her knees against the chill of the air conditioning, Lily sat watching him.

She was porcelain-pale, except where faint bruising still marred her jaw and temple. Her right arm was cradled in a sling. His heart clenched tight. God, how close he'd come to losing her completely.

'Hello,' she said, sending him a watery smile.

It was a slug to the gut. She'd been crying and he knew it was his fault.

'Hello,' he answered, unable to move or remember any of the heartfelt speeches he'd planned to give.

'I'm sorry about the other day,' she said.

'You had every right to kick me out. I understand completely.'

'You do?'

'I offered you a role in my life that was shameful. You think I put you second.'

She chewed on her lip and her free hand plucked at the blanket. Yeah, that was exactly what she'd been thinking.

At last his legs propelled him forward. The Sister had placed the empty chair at least six feet from her precious patient. Well, to hell with that. He dragged it closer, so that when he sat his splayed knees encompassed hers.

She promptly shrank back.

To hell with that, too.

He leant forward, his elbows propped on his knees, and reached for her good hand, gently loosening its grip on the blanket and folding it in both his own.

'How are you?' he asked.

She blinked at him with big owl eyes. 'Getting better, thank you.' She studied their clasped hands. 'Nate said you've been here all the time.'

'I have.'

She peered up at him from beneath her lashes. 'There was no need. You shouldn't feel guilty for what happened.'

'After what you've been through because of me? I don't think I'll ever stop feeling guilty.'

In a small voice she said, 'I thought he was going to kill you. I was so scared.'

The bile rose in his throat. What she'd endured because of him…

'But you prevented it,' he said, squeezing her hand.

'Are you safe now? From the Hyde-Wallaces, I mean?'

'Yes. George's sons don't share his ambitions. Just as well.' His voice gained a menacing edge. 'I'd have crushed them all for what he did to you.'

She shuddered.

He'd frightened her.

He changed the subject. 'The doctors tell me you can leave tomorrow.'

She nodded, keeping her eyes downcast. 'They've arranged therapy for me in London, and a serviced apartment to convalesce in until I'm fit enough to go home.'

He didn't tell her that those arrangements had been made at his order and his expense. Even the 'apartment', which in reality was a penthouse in a luxurious Chelsea development, with every conceivable comfort and convenience she could need and medical staff on call, even though he hoped none of them would be needed.

'That's good,' he said. 'But I may have another option for you to consider.'

She tensed.

'No,' he swiftly reassured her. 'Not that.'

She watched him, wary and fey, as if she might

slip from his grasp and dissolve on the slightest breeze.

Instinctively he drew her hand closer. This time she didn't resist.

*Now,* he thought, *ask her now.*

He took a steadying breath. 'I should begin by saying I don't deserve you. Certainly not after the way I've treated you, and not after what you've gone through because of me. But I have a question to ask. Though I must insist you don't give me your answer tonight. I want you to think of the consequences of saying yes. If that's what you decide. You may say no, of course, and that would be okay, too. Well, obviously not for me...'

Her pale brow creased in confusion.

Not surprising. Had a man ever made such a hash of proposing?

'What I mean is...' He paused, took another breath. 'Lily, will you marry me?'

She gave the tiniest gasp, but her fingers within his remained motionless. That didn't seem good. What if Nate had misjudged her feelings? What if she really couldn't forgive him?

He blundered on. 'I know I have no right to ask you. It's a selfish act. God knows, it's not an easy life. I should let you go.'

But then, oh, then his heart leapt. He felt her fingers move against his.

'What if you're what I want?' she said.

He raised his eyes to hers. Pale grey to determined hazel. And he dared to hope. But she had to understand that often her life would be hard.

'Perhaps what you want isn't good for you?' he said.

'I think it's for me to be the judge of that, don't you?'

Inside, he gave a crow of triumph. There she was. His fierce Lily.

'I know that you'll be good for me. Your stepbrother has already threatened violence if I don't take care of you, but it seems to be the other way round. You keep saving me,' he said. 'That summer, when I arrived in England, I wasn't sure how I was going to get through the next hour, let alone the rest of my life. But you...' He slid his thumb back and forth across her knuckles. 'A little kid, with a big heart, you showed me there was a way.'

She was watching him intently now. Waiting for more. For the words he knew she wanted— no, *needed* to hear. But after all that had happened how did he say them? The words he'd never said out loud before.

How did he tell he loved her?

He looked at their entwined fingers, his large hands engulfing her small one, which somehow looked perfect together.

'Marry her,' his father had said. His parting advice before being discharged from the hospital that morning.

'And inflict this life on her?' Khaled had replied.

The King had laughed. 'I thought the same thing about your mother. But she thrived on it. Lily reminds me of her. The same strength and courage.'

'She told me I should forgive myself.'

'A wise woman. You should listen to her.'

He'd nearly lost his father twice now, and still he'd never told him, never said…

'I'm sorry, Papa. I never meant to hurt Faisal.' His voice had cracked. 'He was my brother.'

'Oh, my boy, my boy,' his father had said, gathering him up. 'I've always known that. *Always*. But you would never let me close enough to tell you. We've worried for you so, your mother and I. But Lily's brought you back to us. So marry her. She'll make you happy.' He'd chuckled. 'And she'll drive you crazy, and challenge you in ways that no one else can.'

Hadn't she already done that? Forcing him to see his frailties and errors. Loving him in spite of it. Making him stronger.

Quietly, almost to himself, Khaled said now, 'My father is right. My mother understood from the start. I just never knew this was how it could be.'

Faisal was gone. Nothing could alter that. But to live a half-life as penance was an insult to his memory. This was the debt he owed his brother and his father: to live the best life he could.

It was time to forgive himself and embrace all that life had to offer.

To embrace love.

He raised his head, looked into the eyes of this incredible woman and felt a seismic shift, a sense of absolute rightness. Suddenly the words were easy.

'I'm yours,' he said, simply. 'I've been yours since the day you first put your hand in mine and led me out of that library. Perhaps I didn't know it then, but I know it now. I love you, Lily. Whatever stupid, dishonourable offer I made in the past, don't let that blind you to the truth. I'm in love with you, and I will be to my last breath.'

Whatever reaction he'd expected, it wasn't the one he got.

She dissolved into tears—great, heaving sobs that shook her whole body.

Completely flummoxed, he did the only thing he could think of. He carefully scooped her up and placed her in his lap.

She clung to his shirt as the tears rolled on. 'I'm sorry. I never used to be such a crier, but these days I can't seem to stop.'

He dug a handkerchief from his pocket and presented it to her. 'These are happy tears, though, aren't they?'

The relief, when she nodded, was indescribable.

She blew her nose, then said uncertainly, 'You really want me?'

'*Habiba*, I've been out of mind these past few days, because I thought you'd kicked me out of your life for good.'

'I was just scared,' she whispered.

'Me, too.'

'You were?'

She looked up at him. The violence of her ordeal was still reflected in the bruises to her skin and the shadows in her eyes, but to him she'd never been lovelier.

'Petrified. I knew I was in trouble from the moment you stepped out of that dressing room.'

She gave a weepy chuckle. 'I knew the minute you took your shirt off.'

'Shameless!' he said in mock outrage, pulling her close again, with her head on his shoulder, her hand on his chest.

She sighed in contentment and his heart swelled. But there was more for her to know—more pain he'd have moved mountains to spare her if he could.

'There is something else…'

She hid her face in his neck. 'If it's about my parents' marriage, I already know. George told me.'

Khaled said nothing, just pressed his cheek to her hair, lending her his strength, his love.

'It's okay,' she said. 'They cared for each other in their own way. Maybe not enough, and maybe too much. But that was their life. Not mine. I won't let it determine how I live any more.' She stroked the fabric of his shirt. 'But what happens to us if the truth comes out?'

'My lawyers may have found a loophole in the Constitution that we can use. As you're not Nabhani, they can argue that the constitutional rule doesn't apply. And if it comes out, and the people really can't accept it, then I'll step down in favour of Amal.'

She stared up at him. 'You'd give up the throne for me?'

'In a heartbeat. We'd live as private citizens—though I'd support Amal from the sidelines, of course.'

'And how is Aisha about all this?'

'Relieved to be spared marriage to me. She wants a different future for herself. Her father is furious, and refusing all contact with me, but I have great hopes for the Crown Prince. He's only seventeen, but growing in confidence. He's a reformer like me.'

'You'll be cultivating his friendship, then? He'll help with those water rights you need?'

'Yes, ma'am,' Khaled said, rewarding his newest advisor with a kiss.

And then they talked. About nothing of great importance. His favourite food. Her favourite films. Books they'd both read. Simple, homely things, but so important to heal them both.

Finally he spoke of Faisal. And for the first time in years he spoke of him without pain. Sharing the memories he had of him. Marvelling again at how Lily had the power to bring him such peace.

They spoke until the sun disappeared and the stars came out and Lily's head began to nod against him. Then he called for the nurses, saw her put to bed, and at last took his leave.

The day outside was blisteringly hot. Lily indulged in a moment's sympathy for the news teams Khaled said were camped out below.

'Whatever you decide,' he'd told her last night, 'I promise I'll always try to protect you from their intrusion.'

Curled up in his arms, with the strong beat of his heart against her cheek, she'd believed him. She'd never felt so safe, so cherished.

That had been just before he'd left. He'd been serious about her taking time to consider his proposal.

'But I can tell you now—' she'd said.

He'd pressed a finger to her lips. 'No. You must think about it and tell me tomorrow.'

Then, with a sweet, lingering kiss, he'd gone. Leaving the hospital for the first time since they'd both entered it over a week ago.

It had taken her all of ten seconds to decide. Whatever her life as a royal consort might hold, once she knew he loved her—he *loved* her—she'd had no doubts.

And today she was going back to the palace— going home, to be with Khaled.

'Good morning, *habiba*.'

The thought of him had conjured the man in the flesh. She heard his soft tread as he crossed the room behind her.

His lips brushed her hair. 'Did you sleep well?' he asked.

She nestled into his shoulder, reaching round to capture a hand and draw it about her waist. His returned caress was gentle, careful of her healing shoulder, of her arm still in its sling.

'Yes,' she replied, actually answering a different question entirely.

'Oh? Was there nothing you had to think about?'

'Yes, but it was all rather pleasant.'

'Pleasant? Might I allow myself to be encouraged by that?'

He'd moved the heavy fall of her hair aside so he could press kisses behind her ear. She shuddered in delight, tipping her head to give him greater access. 'Yes, I think perhaps you might.'

A ripple of tension left his body. He hadn't been sure of her answer, then.

'You look practically edible in this dress,' he murmured against her skin.

It was the one she'd tried that day at the store. She'd requested it be sent from the palace. Along with one or two other items.

'How am I going to keep my hands off you?'

Before she could ask why he saw the need to, he tipped her face up to his with his fingertips.

'But I'll allow myself this,' he said, slanting

his mouth across hers in a kiss so filled with the promise of everything to come that Lily swooned against him.

The next instant he lifted his head. The Sister had entered, with a hospital porter pushing a wheelchair.

Lily frowned at it. 'I don't need that. I'm perfectly capable of walking.'

'Your Highness, Miss Marchant is still recovering, and under no circumstances should she walk out of the hospital.'

'For once, madam, you and I agree,' he said, and swept Lily up in his arms.

She squeaked in protest.

'I know. You can take care of yourself,' Khaled said as he bore her away. 'But will you please learn to accept my help sometimes, woman?'

'Yes,' she said, smiling. 'I will.' And she reached out a hand to trail it through the black silk of his hair. How she loved his hair, and the joy of being able to touch him.

He stepped into the lift. 'I've heard you say yes to me several times this morning, and I think I know what you're really saying.'

She gazed beatifically up at him,

'Don't distract me,' he scolded, 'I have something more to say. My parents and sisters are waiting at home for you. And Nate, too. The press, inevitably, are waiting outside. But I want you to know you can still say no. I've put you through so much. I'm asking you to give up so much. Are you sure I'm what you want?' he asked.

He was looking so uncertain she took his face tenderly in her hands, wanting to banish all his fears. She'd fight dragons for this man.

'You may be a grumpy workaholic, and in my experience far too bossy and autocratic…' His expression clouded over. 'But I'm yours,' she added quickly. 'I've been yours since the very first moment I saw you in my stepfather's library. I knew it then. I've always known it. I'm in love with you and I will be to my last breath. So, yes, I couldn't be more sure.'

They'd arrived at the foyer. As he crossed to the exit his expression softened. The anxiety faded and the most delicious crinkles formed at the corners of his eyes. Another step and the doors to the entrance were swept wide, revealing them at last to the banks of photographers and waiting news crews.

And as the massed cameras went crazy, suddenly there it was. More dazzling, more breathtaking than any photograph. Because the whole force of it was focused on her alone.

A smile.

The smile.

*His* smile.

Oh, wow. She'd happily devote entire weeks of her life trying to coax that from him again.

He halted on the steps.

'Ladies and gentlemen, allow me to officially present Miss Lily Marchant.' His smile widened as he gazed down at her. 'Who has just done me the great honour of consenting to be my wife.'

Bombarded with congratulations and questions, Lily obliged the cameras and reporters with a few waves and smiles of her own until they were moved back by Rais and his team and Khaled, still beaming, strode through it all, carrying his precious burden to the waiting limo.

'Well, that was an experience.' Lily laughed, as the car pulled away.

'Are you okay?'

Khaled was mindful that this was her first time outside the hospital since the attack, and only her second experience of a press pack. Though she'd handled it with aplomb...

He narrowed his eyes on her. 'Did you actually just pose for them?'

She twinkled at him. 'My mother was an actress. It must be in my genes.'

'Lily, the truth about your parents' marriage may still come out. It may not all be easy from here.'

She stopped his explanation with a kiss.

'I know,' she answered. 'But as long as I have you I'll get through it.

She'd slid closer, and her fingers were in his hair again.

Damn, that felt good. But he'd done some hard thinking last night. He'd treated her shamefully from start to finish and he'd vowed to make it up to her. They'd be married soon, but before then he'd woo her properly—and that started with a little restraint on his part.

He captured her hand, kissed it, then placed it firmly back in her lap.

'I thought we could marry at the end of next month. In five weeks. Until then you'll be staying in the waterfront penthouse. We'll go on dates, and I'll visit, of course, but only when Nate or my mother is present to chaperon.'

There. Boundaries clearly established.

'Dates? I see…' she said demurely—which, he'd realise later, should have made him deeply suspicious.

She tapped at the window. 'No one can see us in here, can they?'

'What? No, the glass is one-way,' he answered, distracted by her meek acceptance of his plans.

'And they can't hear us?'

'Only the driver and front seat passenger when you use that intercom button.'

She pressed it.

'Rais?'

'Yes, madam?'

'His Highness would like to take the scenic route home. The one that takes…ooh…let's say about half an hour.'

'The thirty-minute scenic route?' Khaled heard the suppressed laughter of his security chief. 'Of course, madam.'

She lifted her finger from the button.

'Oh, dear. Looks like we're stuck in here for a while, and without a chaperon.' She walked her fingers up his thigh. 'I guess we're just going to have to improvise.'

'Lily.' He caught her wrist. 'We won't be doing any *improvising* until after we're married.'

She actually pouted at him. It was adorable. How was he going to keep his hands off her for five minutes, never mind five weeks?

'Well, that doesn't quite work for me,' she said, watching him with lambent eyes. 'Perhaps I can change your mind?'

His heart stuttered as she did a little shimmy, hitching her dress up her thighs. He caught a flash of her panties.

Tiny. Pink. With pearls and a bow.

*The Bridegroom-Slayer.*

He was done for.

She straddled his lap.

'What about your injuries?' he said, desperately searching for something to firm up his resolve whilst a certain part of his anatomy was enthusiastically firming up all on its own.

'This hand works fine.' She waggled the free one at him, then demonstrated how fine it was by unbuttoning his shirt and exposing his chest to her hungry gaze.

As her fingers dropped lower, found his fly and freed him, he tried to say *Stop*, but it came out more as a strangled, *'Ohh...'*

'Now,' she said, squeezing her hand around him, 'about these five weeks of abstinence...'

His head fell back as he moaned his pleasure. 'But I was going to woo you properly.'

'What if I prefer being wooed improperly? Don't you think this is much nicer?'

She lifted herself up, pushing the thong to one side before sinking back down and taking him inside her.

He was panting now. 'What is it with you and the back seat of limos?'

'It's not the car.' She feathered kisses along his jaw. 'It's the man. He's as sexy as hell. Now, stop talking and make love to me.'

'I'll never be fully in control of anything again, will I?' he groaned, finally surrendering and lifting his hips to thrust into her.

'Perhaps not,' she answered a little breathlessly, 'but imagine all the fun you're going to have.'

Apart from her bare thighs and rucked-up hem, her dress and hair were otherwise pristinely in place. He, however, was a mess. His shirt and trousers were half off, and his hair was probably sticking out in all directions. He suspected she'd step from this car a little flushed, but otherwise as neat as a pin. Whereas he, even after he'd tidied himself, would look exactly what he was: seduced and thoroughly ravished.

*My God,* he thought, *this woman.*

And a bubble of laughter and happiness rose up, exploding like a starburst inside him. He was smiling as she bent her head to kiss him.

'See,' she said. 'You're enjoying yourself already.'

The scenic route back to the palace was, indeed, spectacularly scenic, and the limousine, travelling at an unusually sedate pace, gave the occupants of the back seat every opportunity to enjoy the view.

But neither noticed any of it.

Lily and her very *happy* prince were otherwise occupied. Improvising all the ways she could make him smile. Again and again and again…

\* \* \* \* \*

*If you fell in love with*
Desert Prince's Defiant Bride
*be sure to watch out for*
*Julieanne Howells's next story.*

*Coming soon!*